Scoundrels
of
Skaguay

MARTIN STROUD

Woodcarver Press
Seattle   ▪   Memphis
Copyright © 2019 Martin Stroud
All rights reserved.
ISBN: 978-0-578-51998-2
Library of Congress Control Number: 2019908108

For Pat & Roy; Omar & Sweetie

PROLOGUE

Anyone who happened to pass the small shop on the Seattle waterfront that cold, damp evening might have assumed the small man wrestling with a large metal container by the front door was just closing up for the night. They surely could not have seen the other person.

The morning newspaper would report one person died in the tragic fire that engulfed the location. Locals would mourn the death saying, "he was a nice little man ..." but then would quickly go about the business of the living.

An investigation would yield no concrete evidence pertaining to the origins of the fire; most were just thankful it didn't spread to other buildings on the pier. Yes, it was unfortunate that one person died but no further inquiries would be made.

CHAPTER 1

I packed what few belongings I thought might be important into a canvas bag and put on my bravest face while saying goodbye to my teary mother and sisters. This separation would be for the best but it was sure hard to leave them behind.

The walk to the train depot in the neighboring town of Cle Elum took me about an hour. When finally I saw the whitewashed railroad depot rising up beside the tracks I realized I had taken some first big steps away from my family. I felt grownup and young at the same time. I told myself to be bold.

People were milling about on the platform and I could see the puffing iron horse about fifty yards down the track, idling while filling up from a huge water tank. I realized I also was thirsty and walked over to the well pump to refill my canteen.

I'd spent my entire life watching the trains load and haul coal away from the Roslyn mines, but had never actually ridden the rails myself, so when the engine finished taking on water and slowly lurched forward, I suddenly realized, *this is it, I'm on my way*. With a screech and a huge blast of vapor the train stopped in front of the small platform and the waiting passengers shuffled forward. My first adventure–on my own–was about to begin!

I chose a seat and settled down next to a window, anxious to view everything while we chugged along.

Mama had given me enough money for the fare and a few extra

dollars so I could get a meal or two in Seattle while I searched for Uncle Arthur. I assumed his fishing fleet would be easy enough to find—I would just go to the waterfront and ask around.

"Hey there, young fellow, where you off to?" a white-haired lady sitting across from me asked. She had a hard-sided suitcase and a basket that smelled awfully good.

"I'm going to Seattle to get a job on my uncle's fishing boat—or boats rather. He has a fleet of them!"

"Oh my goodness, young man, that is quite the journey you are commencing." Her kind smile reminded me of my mama. "Perhaps you could help me eat some of my basket lunch; my daughter-in-law isn't the best of cooks but there is plenty to share." I supposed she could tell I was hungry.

"Thank you, ma'am. My name is Henry Dunhill and I'm from Roslyn," I stood up and offered my hand.

"Pleasure to meet you Henry Dunhill. I'm Fern Rose, from Cle Elum originally, but now I live over the pass in a small town called Gilman. I was visiting my son and his wife here as they just had a new baby … my first grandbaby." She removed the white cloth napkin from atop the basket and began to sort through its contents. "Have you traveled much?"

"No ma'am, this is my first trip ever on a train. It's my first trip ever to anywhere for truth."

Mrs. Rose had pulled out a small tin of cookies and struggled with the lid. "Here Henry, you deal with this while I get out the chicken."

I certainly was hungry and I made quick work of the lid. Inside were a dozen or so delicious smelling sugar cookies. It was a challenge to my manners not to dig right in and devour them right then and there.

"Here you go, ma'am," I said as I passed the tin back over to her. "Those look mighty delicious with all that sugar on them."

"Why don't you start with one while I get us set up with this chicken?"

At first look, that basket didn't seem to be that large, but food just kept coming out of it: hard boiled eggs, a dill pickle for each of us, four big pieces of fried chicken, the cookies of course, and, there was even an entire cherry pie! That basket was like a magician's box! I wouldn't have been surprised if Mrs. Rose had pulled a live rabbit out by the end of our meal; it was that spectacular! It seemed like only a matter of minutes before I was truly stuffed out to my shirt buttons.

"Oh my ma'am, that was a most delicious and generous meal! I thank you for your kindness."

"My dear, I am happy I was able to share with you. The good book says to share and share alike, so you remember old Mrs. Rose the next time you have more bounty than you can use—I know you will, you're a fine young man; I can see your folks raised you up right." She smiled at me. I don't remember even closing my eyes.

CHAPTER 2

*I*n a low crouch, hands at the ready, I take the shallowest of breaths as I close in on my target. Creeping forward ever so slowly, I'm confident that my unsuspecting prey stands no chance against my masterful, stealthy approach. Suddenly his head jerks toward me, and I'm caught in his beady gaze. For a moment, I stand frozen.

But I am within striking distance. My eyes narrow intently, holding his stare while I summon my own lightning-quick reflexes. I bend my knees a bit more, shift my weight to the balls of my feet, and I lunge! Squawk!!

My body skids across the ground kicking up a blinding cloud of dust. I gather my arms tightly, determined to keep a firm grasp on … chicken feathers and gravel.

The old Brown Leghorn clucks from across the pen, taunting me. I scramble to my feet and race toward the chicken. Mama has told me to catch supper, and that is just what I intend to do. The chicken bolts again and I dig in my heels to change direction. I'm breathing heavy as I prepare for another approach: bird versus boy. Bird fearing for its life, me hellbent on catching today's meal.

A light rain begins to fall. It will keep the dust down, but no one wants to be slopping around a muddy chicken pen in a rainstorm. I wipe a sleeve across my face, all the time keeping eyes on my skittish prey.

With a burst of speed, I make a beeline for the feathered devil. When I'm just a few feet away, I pull up short, feint left, then dive back to my right. Again I fall on my face and come up empty-handed. This time my elbow scrapes across a jagged rock, and I look down to see that I am bleeding. I'm losing a battle with a

5

creature whose brain is the size of my thumbnail.

Sprawled on my stomach, I scan the perimeter of the fence, but I don't see the chicken anywhere. As I begin to push myself up, I sense something to my left. I turn my head, and there he is. Just standing there mere inches from my face … staring at me. I slowly reach toward my suddenly still foe, then clamp my fist tightly around his skinny neck. And that's when I hear the explosion. A tremendous boom in the distance that rattles buildings, shakes trees, and sends a tremor through the earth beneath me that I feel pulsate through my chest.

I jerked awake, lifting my hand to feel the side of my head that had thunked against the window. The hot July sun beat down on me through the pane of glass I'd been using as a pillow. In the heat of this railroad car, my thick mop of hair felt like some furry critter had taken up residence on my scalp. I looked around and saw that Mrs. Rose was gone. All of the other passengers appeared to be caught up in their own thoughts.

The klick-klack of the train in motion—coupled with a full belly—had lulled me to sleep, and my mind had drifted to the place it so often does when I doze off. I'd chased that stupid chicken around our yard, on and off, for the past five years. Sometimes I caught it, sometimes I didn't. But the dream always ended the same way things had on that awful afternoon.

In our little mining town of Roslyn, Washington, everyone knew the explosion in the distance signalled something bad. Initial reports were that fourteen coal miners had been killed, but it wasn't too long before we learned that the true number was forty-five dead. When my father and my older brother, George Jr., didn't make it home for supper that night, we Dunhills knew what the mining company would confirm two days later: the worst mining disaster in Washington state history had buried both of my family's adult males nearly 2000 feet underground.

Mama cooked chicken that night, though none of us had any appetite. Seated at the kitchen table with my two younger sisters and my mother, I grappled with the idea that I, eleven-year-old Henry

Dunhill, was now the man of the house. The only sounds in the room were three of us chewing and Mama sobbing into her plate.

The Northern Pacific Coal Company paid out one thousand dollars to each of the women widowed by the explosion. Mama, always the frugal sort, worked hard to keep our family afloat. We three kids went to school and Mama took in washing each week from some of the town's more prosperous families. But money for the Dunhills just kept getting scarcer, and by the time I turned sixteen, neighbors had begun to gossip that a person my age was a man and ought to be doing more to support his family. Many boys I knew had already been forced to quit school to get jobs in the coal mines but Mama said she'd be damned if she was gonna lose another son to that deadly business. But even she knew something had to change if our family was going to survive.

One night, after dinner, she told me I should go to Seattle to get a job working for her brother, Arthur. He'd left Roslyn for the big city years earlier, and Mama had gotten a letter in the mail from him the previous Christmas saying he had his own fishing business in Seattle with a whole fleet of boats. Since I didn't rightly recall much about him, Mama described him as "not the worst person in the world." He had told her back then, if we ever needed anything, we should look him up. And we were in pretty desperate need right then.

CHAPTER 3

All the hours on the train had given me time to think—and worry. What would life be like in Seattle? Would I be able to hold my own? I'd never even seen the ocean much less been on a fishing boat such as I imagined Uncle Arthur would have. I just had to have faith that my prospects over the mountain would be good because staying in Roslyn would mean I'd have to go into the mines like my father and brother had. No, Seattle was my future, I had to find my way. Everyone was counting on me.

I must admit my first view of the city was pretty shocking. I'd never traveled past the hills around Roslyn and Cle Elum. Sure, we had tall trees and lakes, but never had I seen such a large body of water or so many people as I did in Seattle. The train wound its way over many bridges and one time it seemed as if we were dangerously floating over the huge bay itself. I could have sworn I saw fish right outside my train car window.

"Final stop, Elliott Bay! Railroad Avenue at Columbia Street! Everyone disembark, please!" a man in an official-looking blue jacket called out.

I watched absentmindedly as my fellow passengers began collecting their things in preparation for our arrival. I thought it was lucky that the train stopped right near the waterfront—I wouldn't have to walk far to find Uncle Arthur's fleet of boats.

With a mighty screech the train jerked to a stop and I leaned down to pick my bag up from beneath my feet. I couldn't help but smile when I saw that Mrs. Rose had left the tin of cookies by my bag. I quickly popped off the lid and reached in for another sugary treat. On top of the last three cookies, there was a slip of paper. Written in a spidery hand were the words: *Watch your step Henry Dunhill.* She had signed it with a picture—a fern frond and a rose bud.

Watch your step?

I joined the queue headed for the exit doors and, abiding by Mrs. Rose's advice, carefully stepped onto the platform. I was greeted by the throaty caw of countless sea gulls circling above, and the hustle-bustle of business up and down the street. A strong breeze blew in off the water, and I felt cool for the first time since I'd begun my trip. I breathed in deeply, tasting salty sea air.

As the activity on the platform thinned out, I took a long look around to get my bearings. I felt around for my father's pocket watch—my pocket watch—saw that it was around 5:00 p.m., and decided to get a move on and start looking for Mama's brother. I figured a big-time fishing operation like Uncle Arthur's was bound to be at one of the busier piers along the waterfront. From the looks of things, those were mostly to the north of where I stood. I hefted my bag onto my shoulder and started along Railroad Avenue.

CHAPTER 4

The sun was low in the western sky but the sunlight glinting off the water caused me to shield my eyes whenever there was a break in the storefronts. And so many stores there were: boating supplies, rope and sailmakers, blacksmiths, barrels stacked high, fishing gear, stand-up eateries, and most surprisingly a shop that had a skeleton waving at me from the front window! I walked slowly, gawking at the endless variety of merchandise. Hawkers held up dried fish, sausages, even packages of some type of colorful candy concoctions.

The sidewalks were so crowded that a person couldn't take a full stride like back home; in Seattle I needed to take little steps and keep my eyes focused on the way ahead. After a few blocks, I found my path obstructed by a large cluster of men who had congregated in front of a wooden storefront.

To make my way around the group, I stepped all the way out to where the railroad tracks ran down the center of the dusty avenue. Through the cloud of cigar smoke that hovered above the men, I was able to make out a carved wooden sign that said *Godfrey Oyster Market*.

When the whistle of an approaching engine sounded, I quickly scuttled back to the safety of the boardwalk.

At the next corner, I saw steps leading down to a floating dock. I looked to my left at the side of a yellow-slatted building to see if it offered any clues as to where I was. Bold, red letters against a blue background said *Hitchens Pier*. Tied up alongside was a sturdy looking vessel, painted white, with a single smokestack in the middle. Three men in uniforms were on board, and as I watched them I heard a sweet voice call from behind me.

"Excuse me, sir."

I turned to see a pretty girl, perhaps a year or two older than I, in a checkered blue dress. I couldn't make out what she said next because her words were drowned out by the din of the locomotive that chugged down the tracks directly behind her.

"I beg your pardon?" I leaned in.

"Can I trouble you for the time?" she asked meekly.

"Oh, sure!" I said, happy to know I could be of some assistance. I switched my bag over to my left shoulder and fumbled in my right pocket for my watch. As I raised it up to check the time, I was jarred by a collision with a passerby.

"Hey, watch it, rube," the angry fellow growled at me. As I turned to apologize, another man collided with me and knocked me to the ground. My bag cushioned my fall a bit, but I was so embarrassed to have clumsily fallen in front such a lovely miss. I'd have to be more careful. A guy could get hurt just trying to tell someone what time it—

I felt my pocket. Nothing. I looked around where I'd fallen. Nothing. My pocketwatch was gone … and so was the girl.

A man from a fire boat crew had witnessed my tumble and came up to see if I was okay. I considered asking him if he could just help me onto the very next train back to Cle Elum, but instead I said, "I'm looking for my Uncle Arthur … uh, Arthur Torkelson, that is."

"Nah, sorry, I don't know any Arthur Tor—" he stopped abruptly. "Wait … do you maybe mean Artie Torkelson?"

"Um … maybe."

"Well, if it's Artie Torkelson you seek, by this time of day, it's a safe bet that you'll find him at *The Lucky Break*. You know where that is?"

I admitted that I had no idea where anything was. He instructed me to go back toward the train platform then, when I reached Norwegian Bank and Trust, make a left up the hill. I thanked him and turned to walk south.

From what Mama had told me, Uncle Arthur had been very fortunate to have invested his meager savings into a successful fishing vessel. She was proud of him for making good in the city, even though he had previously only fished on the small lakes around their childhood home. Based on the way the fireman had said Uncle Arthur's name, however, I'd begun to worry that things might not be as they seemed.

I jostled my way through a sea of people who all seemed to be heading the opposite direction. I wasn't sure where everyone was going, but I thought perhaps this was what it felt like to be a salmon fighting against a powerful current to reach its destination upstream.

CHAPTER 5

In the fading light, I rounded the corner onto First Avenue and began looking for the pool hall called *The Lucky Break*. Most everything on the block was overshadowed by a colossal brick hotel where a doorman was helping a fancy couple out of a horse-drawn carriage. Clearly there were people arriving in Seattle who rated a much warmer welcome than I'd received.

When the doorman returned to his place back in front of the glass doors, I took the opportunity to ask him about the pool hall. He flicked his thumb across the street where, indeed, hung a small tin sign saying, *The Lucky Break*.

I tugged open the door and was surprised to see that the rickety little sign out front wasn't anything like the interior! Much of the huge room was dimly lit, but I did see a string of lights swinging over the green felt of four pool tables. Once my eyes adjusted, I saw that men were seated at tables all along the walls to my right and left. In a dim back corner was a group of fellows playing darts.

Busy gawking at the buzz of activity in the pool hall, I was startled when someone tapped me on the shoulder and asked, "You need help with something?"

I turned to see a fellow, about my age but much taller, who had bright red hair, and ears that stuck out a little too far. He was wearing red suspenders and a red bowtie.

"You work here?" I asked.

13

"Yep. Since before I could even see over the pool tables. Name's Silas," he said as he extended his hand.

"Good to meet you Silas. My name's Henry. Henry Dunhill. I just got into town today."

"I figured as much. Not too many locals show up here with their luggage." he said with a grin, nodding toward the bag I was still lugging over my shoulder.

"Oh, I guess not," I said. "Well, maybe you can help me. I'm looking for my uncle. He's a fisherman in town and a guy down by the pier said I was likely to find him here. His name's Arthur—or Artie—Torkelson."

Silas suddenly looked perplexed. "Artie Torkelson's your uncle?"

"Yeah, my mother's brother. He used to live near us in Roslyn but I haven't seen him since I was a little kid. I'm not really sure that I'd recognize him. D'you know if he's here?"

Silas looked to one of the pool tables, biting his bottom lip as if trying to solve a puzzle. Then he looked over his shoulder to the other side of the room where a polished wooden bar ran along the wall. The bartender, wearing the same suspenders and bowtie as Silas, looked in our direction, smiled and gave Silas a nod.

"You've come to the right place, Henry. Artie Torkelson is at that last table over there," Silas pointed.

"Oh great! I finally caught a lucky break," I joked.

Silas gave a good natured chuckle. "Artie's the one in the striped shirt."

"Thanks Silas. I appreciate it."

"Don't mention it," he said. "Mighty good meeting you Henry."

Silas walked toward the bar, and I made my way to the pool table to find my uncle. The men gathered around the table seemed pretty engrossed in the game at hand. I noticed a sizeable pile of cash stacked just behind one of the corner pockets.

Hesitantly, I said, "Excuse me, I'm looking for Arthur Torkelson."

No one acknowledged me, so I thought perhaps I needed to speak up. I cleared my throat and tried again, louder this time. "Excuse me.

Is one of you Arthur, or Artie, Torkelson?"

The man in a striped shirt, lining up his pool cue for a shot, raised his eyes long enough to say, gruffly, "No one by that name here kid. Eight ball, corner pocket, boys!"

I was confused, but then I saw that there was another man in a striped shirt playing cards at a small round table near where the cue sticks hung on the wall. I made my way around the pool table and squeezed past the man who was leaning down, eye level with the rail. Suddenly, I was jolted by a sharp pain in my side. The man spun around to face me, bug-eyed, nostrils flared.

The fury on the face was made all the worse by its familiarity, this was my mother's brother all right and he was spitting mad.

"Dammit! You don't EVER get in the way when I'm lining up a shot!" he snarled, pounding the end of his cue stick to the floor.

"I'm so sorry. I was j-j-just lookin' for—"

"Yeah, yeah. Arthur Torkelson. I'm Arthur Torkelson. Who the devil are you?!"

His face was inches from mine and I bore the brunt of breath noxious enough to kill a herd of cattle.

"I'm Henry. Henry Dunhill, your nephew from Roslyn." I stammered.

"Roslyn?! That backwards turd of a town?"

I didn't understand why Uncle Arthur would be so rude about the town where he'd grown up, but it turned out that the insults were only beginning.

"You told Mama that if we was ever to need help, to find you. So that's what I've been trying to do. I don't have much experience, but I'm a real quick learner. I'm sure I could help you out on one of your fishing boats if someone will just show me the ropes."

"Fishing boats?" came a voice from the far end of the pool table. I looked up to find the source of the question and saw that some men had gathered 'round to hear. "Artie has fishing boats?"

"Yes," I explained to no one in particular. "I came to Seattle to find work on one of my uncle's fishing boats."

As soon as I said this, the sea of faces around me erupted in laughter.

"That's ripe! The only time Artie sets sail is when he's three sheets to the wind!!" a lanky fellow howled.

More laughter boiled from the crowd, but I saw quite a different reaction from Uncle Arthur. His face was almost purple and his jaw was tightly clenched.

Confused, I pleaded, "It doesn't have to be a great job, but Mama says any job is better than going into the mines."

"Look here, runt," Arthur said, poking a stubby, blue-chalked finger in my chest, "if my sister was so interested in my help, she woulda heeded my words when I told her not to marry that loser of a coal miner."

I'm still not certain whether Uncle Arthur lost his balance or lunged at me on purpose, but whichever it was, the resulting shove drove me back into the wall. Arthur also fell to the floor, drawing even more howls from the crowd.

I felt paralyzed. Anger and hurt collided in my chest and lodged in my throat, my vision blurred and I felt something wet roll down my cheek. Coming here had been a terrible mistake. I was just a fool.

Arthur grunted as he tried to get up. He shook off the fall and refocused his attention on me. I looked around, trying to see the clear path to the door, to get out and never return. But, before I could take a single step, Uncle Arthur had drawn back his fist to take a swing at me.

I turned my head, and closed my eyes bracing for the impact, but the punch never landed. From behind my upraised hands I took a peek and saw Arthur floating away from me, his arms and legs flailing as two men in bow ties and suspenders carried him toward the front door.

CHAPTER 6

"Let me get us a couple of drinks to go with that," Silas said. He walked over to the bar, leaving me alone at a small table with the plate of steamed clams and boiled potatoes that a kindly woman had brought from the kitchen. Although insisting that they shouldn't go to any trouble, once the food was put in front of me I realized I hadn't eaten anything since the train ride that morning and was very hungry.

The woman must have sensed that it was my first time eating clams because she patiently demonstrated how to remove them from their shells and dip them in the cup of melted butter. They were very chewy and some were quite gritty but dipped in butter they were just fine by me.

Across the room, Silas chatted with the bartender, then returned with two frosty mugs.

"A toast," Silas said, hoisting his own glass, "on behalf of the great city of Seattle, a warm welcome to our newest arrival. Please excuse those on the welcoming committee who were lacking in social graces."

Hesitantly, I raised my frothy beverage and clinked glasses with Silas. I smiled uneasily as I watched Silas take a gulp. Through pursed lips, I took the tiniest possible sip of my drink. Cold and sweet, it was not at all what I'd expected. Silas must have seen the perplexed look on my face, because after he'd taken his second gulp, he wiped his mouth on his sleeve, and announced, "Sarsaparilla!"

I gave a sigh of relief. "So … root beer?" I had never had a drink of sarsaparilla.

"Pretty much. Wait … were you thinkin' *The Lucky Break* makes a habit of getting newcomers drunk?"

"Well, I don't rightly know what I was thinking. The whole world seems a bit topsy-turvy at the moment," I laughed.

"I can tell you that Nick over there would have none of that in his establishment," Silas said, casting a thumb in the direction of the bow-tied bartender who had helped Silas rescue me only moments earlier. "Besides, I'm pretty sure Artie done drank all the alcohol on the premises."

Silas asked me what had led to my seeking work opportunities with such an upstanding citizen as Arthur Torkelson. As I told him my story I kept thinking that surely Silas would find my tale of small town woe to be pathetic and dull.

When I confessed that, not even one full day into my grand adventure, I already missed my mother something awful, Silas told me that he had no memory of his mother.

"Yep, from what I understand, she skipped town the day before my second birthday," Silas said. "No one's heard from her since."

"Oh … I'm sorry"—I felt foolish for complaining about my own situation—"And here I was …"

"Don't be silly, Henry," Silas said reassuringly, "if you had a mom and didn't miss her, that's when I'd say you was some real gullyfluff."

We laughed and before long we were swapping stories like we'd known each other forever. I learned that Nick had a soft spot for Silas. He and Silas' dad had been friends since childhood in Seattle. Nick and Earl had worked together as sawyers at Yesler's Mill until the day of the tragic accident that claimed Earl's life. Silas was only six years old when he became an orphan and was forced to live with his wretched Aunt Edna who, other than providing a flea-ridden mattress for sleeping, pretty much left her young nephew to fend for himself. But it was Nick—always Nick—who looked out for Silas.

Just after the Seattle fire of 1889 wiped out most everything including Yesler's Mill, Nick joined in the rebuilding of the city and went all in with his tavern and pool hall and Silas had been a fixture there since the day it opened for business.

After a while, Silas noticed the size of the crowd clamoring for drinks at the bar had grown much larger.

"Henry, I gotta get back to work to help Nick keep up with this mob," he said. Behind the bar, Nick was busy pumping two beers at once. As I watched my new red-headed friend spring into action to assist Nick behind the bar, the lanky fellow who'd been playing pool with Uncle Arthur approached my table and introduced himself as Walter. He said he was sorry about, but not surprised by, what had happened with Arthur.

"But Artie was right about one thing," he said. "Eight ball did go in the corner pocket."

"Huh?"

"You know, I been playing pool with Artie for years. I've seen him lose many times. He's truly awful at pool," Walter said, shaking his head. "If you hadn't bumped into him, he never would've sunk that shot."

"Um, okay ..." I said, still wondering why Walter was telling me this.

"So, the way I figure it, these winnings rightfully belong to you," Walter said as he dropped a pile of cash right next to my plate.

CHAPTER 7

"So how much did it add up to?" Silas asked as he wiped down the bar.

"A hundred and eighty-five dollars!" I said, still a bit stunned by the turn of events.

Silas whistled. "You see, Seattle ain't all bad!"

"I'd have to say you're right about that," I admitted.

"Hey, we can leave as soon as I tap another keg of Rainier," Silas said. "This stuff sells so fast we can barely keep up."

Silas told me that a fellow he knew was playing piano over at the Ulysses Hotel and invited me to tag along. Since I had no idea where else in Seattle I ought to go, the Ulysses seemed as good a next stop as any.

Seeing Silas wrestling with the keg, Nick said, "Don't worry about that, Silas, I'll take care of it. You two get outta here and have some fun."

"Thanks, Nick!" Silas said. He took off his apron and moved over to hang it on a hook behind the cash register.

Standing next to me at the bar were two stiff-collared types blathering about some place called the Klondike.

"No, Coop, I heard it with my own ears," said the taller man. "The Canadian authorities are requiring that all gold-crazed miners have enough food and equipment with them before allowing them over the passes."

The other man chuckled. "We've got it made! Let's get busy bulking up our inventory to insure we have just what these idiots need … or don't need."

"Oh, I've already contacted our canvas tent supplier and tripled our order."

They toasted each other, downed their whiskey shots and asked Nick how much they owed.

"That'll be fifty cents," said Nick.

"Fifty cents my Aunt Fanny!" sputtered the taller man. "When did the cost of this bilge water go up?" The shorter one tossed two silver dollars onto the bar, and both men walked out laughing. After they were out of earshot I leaned over and asked Nick, "Who are those two fellows?"

"Them two? They own Cooper & Levy, the big hardware store," Nick grumbled. "They sell just about everything a person might need. Yep, already two of the wealthiest men in Seattle and soon to be richer from what I hear. Rich keep getting richer …"

"Geez, doesn't it bother you to have to serve louts like that?" I asked.

"Hey, I gotta make a living—we can't all be this lucky," he said as he tossed the morning edition of The Seattle Post-Intelligencer down in front of us. The headline read: GOLD, GOLD, GOLD.

Silas and I leaned over the paper. The entire front page was filled with news and pictures about a steamship soon to dock in Seattle, filled with Klondike gold.

"Don't that figure," I grumbled. "These guys find some yellow metal in the ground and they're set for life. What luck."

Silas grabbed the paper with both hands and disappeared behind it. After a long moment, he slowly turned his head toward me, a sly grin across his face. He slid the paper over. I looked down and saw his finger resting on a headline that read:

The latest reports from the New Eldorado Arrive this morning—The Recent Strikes Seem to be as Rich as Reported—There is Plenty of Gold, But Only the Hardy and

Provident Can Secure it.

"Well, you are kinda skinny, Henry, but I'm Hardy," Silas said. "Do you suppose you could just be Provident?"

CHAPTER 8

Although I wasn't sure what 'provident' meant, the newspaper did say that "fortune seemed to smile on the inexperienced men ..." and I figured, who was more inexperienced than we were? Silas and I started cooking up a plan.

The idea of prospecting for gold had always appealed to me. I'd read all the dime novels about the Forty-Niners and their gold-seeking adventures in California with my imagination whisking me away from a dreary life to a world where the promise of riches lay at the tip of every shovel.

Silas pointed out that we dang sure weren't going to strike anything in Seattle. No sir, a fellow didn't have any golden opportunities lying under his boots. Our minds swirled with ideas about how we'd soon be living the lives of triumphant gold miners. We were both talking at once and our excitement caught the attention of a nearby bar patron.

"You pups are talking outta your hats. You can't afford to join in this crazy stampede. It says here in the paper that a fella needs at least $800 for all the foul weather gear and food. You two would starve to death even before the snow started to fall." He shook his head and turned back to the bar.

Nick put a fresh one down in front of him and said, "Now you hush up, Dick Beane, these fellows are allowed to dream."

"Yeah, sure, a dream that'll get 'em kilt quicker 'n a rattlesnake strike. I know about gold mining—it's hard work—even in California, where it's warm. In Alaska, you got frozen earth—cold that will turn any living thing into a slab of ice, swarms of mosquitoes that hunt flesh like wolves. "

"That may all be true," Nick said, "but someone's gonna claim that gold and whoever does will be set for life. If Silas and Henry strike it rich, it might spare them having to earn a living slinging drinks for grumpy old coots like you."

Despite Nick's encouraging words, the old timer's words certainly had the effect of dampening our spirits.

"No, Nick, he's right," Silas admitted. "Henry and me would be willing to put in the hard work, but there's no way we'll ever come up with the money needed to get us there."

"Finally, someone talking some sense," said Dick, nodding in agreement. He polished off his drink, paid his bill, and went on his way. We sat in glum silence as Nick served patrons at the far end of the bar.

"Woulda been pretty great, though, huh?" Silas said.

"Without a doubt," I agreed. "But it seems the only way to make lots of money is to have lots of money in the first place. Do you still wanna go see that piano player at the Ulysses?"

"You bet," Silas said. "Hey, Nick! We're taking off. See you tomorrow."

Nick looked up and excused himself from the conversation he was having with one of his customers. "Boys, can I talk to you for a minute?" he said as he walked back over to us.

"Sure thing, Nick," Silas said.

"You know, Silas, if this gold rush had come along when me and your old man were your age," Nick said, "nothin' in the world would've kept us from jumping on the next steamship to Alaska."

Silas gave a sad smile at the mention of his father. "Well, what's stopping you now?" he asked.

"I can't afford to go."

"You neither, huh?" I asked.

24

"Oh, I've got plenty of money. But I've got a wife, a kid, and another kid on the way. I can't afford to leave all that behind. You fellas, though … no wives, no kids? Maybe it's your destiny."

"No wives, no kids," Silas said. "Also not enough money."

"Like I said, Silas. I've got some money. You want to go to the Klondike?"

Our jaws dropped as it dawned on us what Nick was saying. "Tell me how much you need."

The door to the Klondike had just been thrown open wide.

"Gosh, Nick, that's mighty generous of you … but I have no idea how we'd pay you back," Silas said.

Nick smiled and shrugged, "That's easy. I assume you'll pay me back in gold."

"No, Nick, I'm serious," Silas said. "You've already done so much for me; I oughta be the one giving you money."

"Okay, Silas. You've gotta decide what's right for you, but when Yesler's Mill burned down, and I put up all my savings to open this place, people thought I was ding dong crazy. I remember folks saying, 'I thought you had more sense than that Nick. Where you gonna get customers? Most of Seattle is flat broke.'

"But look at this place now." We followed Nick's gaze as he surveyed the crowd packed into *The Lucky Break*. "It's true it was a risk, but do you know how many days I wake up wishing I'd just played it safe and gotten a job at the next closest sawmill?" Nick curved his fingers and thumb together to make the sign for 'zero.'

Silas did his best to act happy on the short walk to the Ulysses, but I could tell that turning down Nick's offer hadn't been as easy for him as he'd wanted me to believe. He seemed to be wrestling with what Nick had said about the hazards of playing it safe.

His subdued mood didn't last long though. As we approached the entrance to the hotel, the doorman beamed. "Silas Sprague! Good to see you, young man. You here to see the Emerald Trio?"

"Sure enough, Scotty. This here's my friend Henry. He's new to Seattle and I promised I'd take him to hear the finest piano-playing this side of the Mississippi."

"Good to meet you Henry, but I'm afraid you won't be hearing any piano tonight. Whole band up and quit. They're going up north to look for gold."

"Now how are they gonna do that?" Silas asked. "If there's anyone in Seattle with less money than me, it's the fellas in that band!"

"Mr. Ulysses, man who owns this here fine establishment, offered to stake any employee who wants to go to the Klondike—so long as they agreed to give him a fifty percent share of all the gold they find."

"That's right generous of him."

"Well, between you and me, I don't think it's so much his generosity as it is his jealousy. You see, Mr. Ulysses has a friend he plays euchre with who just returned on that steamship *Portland*, bragging about his bonanza of $100,000 in gold. Frankly, Silas, I'm surprised you aren't joining in the stampede. Enterprising young man like you probably stands a better chance than a bunch of musicians and card players!"

"Me and Henry plan to be partners in the biggest gold strike anyone's ever seen and Nick offered to give us the money but I said I'd rather wait until I save up my own funds to pay my way."

"You can try that if you like, Silas, but by the time you get up there, I guarantee you every bit of the gold will already be spoken for. This is one of those once-in-a-lifetime opportunities—that gold ain't gonna sit around waiting for you to scrape together enough nickels to make a go of it."

Just then, one of the hotel's brass-trimmed doors came flying open, narrowly missing Scotty who leapt out of the way. A portly fellow, not more than a few years older than Silas and me, burst through the doorway, out of breath.

"Scotty! You'll never believe who just quit his job to go to the Klondike!"

"Aye," Scotty said giving him a dismissive look, "I know, I was telling Silas and Henry here that the band …"

"Not the band, man, the mayor—or should I say 'ex-mayor,' of Seattle hisself is going! He wired his resignation from a meeting in San Francisco."

"No kidding," Scotty said shaking his head. "Folks in Seattle aren't going to be too happy with their mayor."

"Won't make a spit of difference to him. He says he's buying a ship in San Fran and sailing straight to the Klondike, says he don't want to waste one more day in Seattle when all the big money's to be found up north!" The man paused and lit up a cigar.

Silas gave me a look and I nodded. We bid a quick goodbye to the two men and hightailed it back to *The Lucky Break*. We had urgent business to discuss with Nick.

CHAPTER 9

Silas could barely contain his excitement as he explained to Nick that we'd had a change of heart. Nick couldn't resist teasing for just a moment, "Gosh, Silas, I don't know. I was just thinking that I might need that money to fund my campaign."

"Your campaign?"

"Sure, you know I've always kinda thought I'd make a great mayor…." Nick winked at me. He smiled and said, "Just having some fun with you boys. Of course the offer still stands."

With great seriousness, Silas pledged to Nick that this was not to be charity. Nick would be an investor, a partner in the venture who would be entitled to a fifty percent share of all the gold found.

Nick shook his head. "As there are three partners in this venture, I will accept a one-third share of all the gold you find and not one nugget more."

Sensing that Silas wanted the agreement to be completely official, Nick grabbed a copy of the flyer advertising the recently departed Ulysses Hotel band, flipped it over, and wrote out a simple contract. We all signed it, and Nick said he would make the financial arrangements with Cooper and Levy for all the supplies we'd need.

The good news about the fortunate souls on the steamship *Portland* had traveled so fast that when we showed up at Cooper & Levy just after sunup the next day it was already packed full with people of all ages, clogging up the aisles and grabbing at the offered goods.

A harried sales clerk finally turned our way and shoved a printed list of supplies recommended for the journey into Silas' hand. It said we would need a canvas tent, a sled to haul our supplies over snow, thick sweaters, heavy boots, woolen blankets, saws, rope, pickaxes, as well as pounds and pounds of food like bacon, rice, corn meal, canned meats, and all manner of dried fruits.

After nearly two frantic hours in Cooper & Levy, we finally made our purchases by handing over Nick's promissory note. We also made arrangements for our grubstake to be carted down to Schwabacher's Wharf for storage.

"Hey, Silas, how are you feeling?" I inquired of my new friend as we stepped out into the sunlight.

"I can't wait to get going! You ain't havin' second thoughts are you?"

"No, I'm just worried that we may have forgotten something. You think we've got everything we need?"

"Not quite," Silas clapped me on the back. "We can't get to Alaska on foot now can we?"

The ticket office of the Pacific Coast Steamship Company was a few blocks away. The sign in the window advertised *The Only Real Ocean Steamships on the Alaska Route*. Silas pulled open the front door and said, "After you, partner," and motioned me through.

The interior of the office was filled with fidgety travelers; and, as over at Cooper & Levy, I assumed most had the same goal in mind as we did. We got in the shortest ticket line and slowly began inching forward.

"Henry, you've still got Artie's … I mean your cash winnings in your pocket, right?"

"Yeah Silas, same as when you asked me five minutes ago," I tapped my jacket pocket.

"Oh, sorry. I guess I'm just worried that something will go wrong."

We finally reached the front of the line and stepped up to the ticket window. Our noses were immediately bombarded by a smell that was coming from the pudgy ticket agent. He was nearly bald but had the most elaborately waxed, twirly mustache I had ever seen; through it he mumbled words that sounded like 'bear poo.'

I turned to Silas, wondering if perhaps he'd been better able to decipher what the man had said. Seemingly he had not as Silas asked, "Beg your pardon?"

The man looked up slowly with an expression that suggested he'd tasted something rotten and said, "What're you? Deef? I said 'Where to?'"

"We'd like two tickets on the next ship to the Klondike," I said.

"That's $82.50," the man said. He began forcefully stamping papers.

"Um, do you have anything cheaper?" I asked.

"Cheaper?" The man frowned, then replied, "Well, there's 4th class passage. Two tickets for that'll run you $50."

"What's 4th class?" Silas asked.

"You like goats and chickens?" the man asked, a bemused sneer forming.

"Sure … I guess," Silas said.

"Goats and chickens travel 3rd class," the man chuckled as he took fifty dollars and handed us two tickets for passage on the steamship *Klickitat*.

CHAPTER 10

Over the years since his dad's death, Silas had declined many invitations to stay with Nick's family, never wanting to impose. He'd been staying at the YMCA on Fourth Avenue, and that's where I opted to stay for the few nights remaining before our scheduled departure.

I didn't have any possessions beyond what I'd carried with me from Roslyn, but Silas had to figure out what to do with the things he'd accumulated over the years: blankets, pillows, books, a checkerboard, and some clothes that weren't warm enough to bother hauling to the Klondike. He sold what he could to other residents at the YMCA and moved the rest down to the front desk, figuring some other fellow would soon make use of them. The one item Silas did not part with however, was his father's little pepperbox pistol. It was old and had probably never been fired, but Silas shared with me that the tiny gun was dear to his heart as it was his only remaining link to his departed father. I had never seen such a pistol and was fascinated by the etched handle. I admired it for a while before he stowed it away. It probably wouldn't be much good for protection against wild animals in Alaska but it had other powers for Silas.

On our last night in Seattle I sat at a small table in a back corner of *The Lucky Break* and wrote a letter home while Silas worked his final night there:

Dear Mama,

      The train trip was good and the sights were amazing, especially crossing over the mountains! I was able to locate Uncle Arthur pretty soon after I arrived and he's already been more help than he knows. Although things are slow in the fishing business right now, Uncle Arthur made a generous contribution to back a venture that my new pal Silas and I are planning to start very soon. I hope you are doing well. Please tell Ruthie and Margaret Ann that I say hello.

Your loving son,

Henry

I put the letter in an envelope and wrote the address as neatly as I could. I left it with Nick who said he would send it off. With any luck, I could make Mama and the girls rich as well.

Sleep that night was nearly impossible but neither of us was the least bit tired when early the next morning we walked up the gangway and boarded the steamship. We were on our way to find our fortunes in Alaska with the clothes we were wearing, one tiny pistol, and the brand-new gear purchased from Cooper & Levy. We waved at our friend and benefactor who had come down to the pier to wish us luck. There were hundreds of others with the same idea and the dock was as crowded as the deck of the ship as families and friends bid their courageous adventurers farewell. I could hardly believe what was happening. I was traveling to a new and even more wild place and was now Henry Dunhill, Alaska gold seeker.

The *Klickitat* wasn't much to look at and I heard some passengers openly express worry about her seaworthiness but when the steam horn blared and the bells clanged even the most timid among us left such doubts behind. As the water roiled and the crowd roared, I could hardly breathe. More chances and changes were coming my way.

CHAPTER 11

The ticket agent had teased us about goats and chickens, but goats and chickens would have been an improvement over the real smells we had to live with during six long days aboard the ship, there were lots of men and quite a few animals as well sharing the voyage. Dogs, tough looking dogs of every breed and color, used the remaining deck space even though nearly every inch of the deck was stacked high with boxes of precious grubstake cargo. Heavy tarpaulins were lashed as protection from the winds and waves of the sea voyage for boxes and dogs alike.

Everything was interesting to me as I had never been on such a vessel before; in fact I had never even been on the ocean before so I spent lot of time exploring the *Klickitat* and talking with any crew member who would give me the time. I can't say I was very seaworthy as quite a few times I felt sick. The route north, through what's called the inland passage, kept us within sight of land, but the cold sea air still cut like a knife. Even bundled in our newly purchased cold-weather woolen coats, we shivered through the days, and our teeth chattered through the nights. We were landlubbers we decided, but sacrifices had to be made in order to reach our golden destination. We talked, made plans, and listened to our fellow passengers, trying to learn as much as we could from those who had the most experience in the wilderness.

On the last day of our voyage, I awoke at daybreak to find that

Silas wasn't in his bedroll. All the other mornings aboard the ship, he'd still been snoring long after I'd fixed myself some breakfast. I headed up to the main deck to look for him.

It didn't take more than a few seconds to locate my partner and friend. He was the only person on deck who was wearing a ladies' hat!

Silas didn't think it was a ladies' hat. Just before we'd boarded the ship, he'd purchased the hat from a vendor along the pier peddling "the finest in New York fashions." Its mustard yellow color and the extra wide brim drew mockery and wisecracks from some of our fellow travelers, but Silas was unfazed and wore it proudly. He claimed it would 'protect him' from harm and when pulled down over his ears would keep the rain off his neck. Since my first day in Seattle, I had come to see Silas as a good and kindly soul, so who was I to stop him from such a choice? A hat with a pushed up brim wasn't really any more noteworthy than any of the other choices of headwear we had all chosen to keep ourselves warm. I had taken to tying a scratchy, plaid woolen scarf over the top of my hat which gave me the look of a dentist's toothache customer.

I spied the hat near the bow of the ship and made my way over. I called out to Silas, but he didn't turn around. I tapped him on the shoulder, "Hey Silas! What are you doing up so early today?"

His gaze was fixed on the horizon. He reached back, threw his arm over my shoulder and pulled me alongside him at the railing. I looked at him, puzzled.

"Henry … look …" he said, slowly raising a finger to point directly in front of us.

I did look and saw right away what had Silas so mesmerized. The fog had lifted, revealing the most spectacular sight I'd ever beheld. The sun reflected across the green-blue waters of a wide harbor and as we drew closer, the majestic mountains seemed to tumble down to envelop us, their deep green slopes and snow-capped peaks calling. We'd arrived—Alaska.

We were loaded with anticipation but the ship had dropped

anchor far from the docks. It was low tide and salty mudflats surrounded the harbor at our destination, Skaguay.

"How are we going to get all our things over to dry land?" I asked out loud to no one in particular.

A burly deckhand I had come to know as Smasher (he was missing a few fingers on his left hand) shook his head and muttered, "Too dumb to live. Yer just gonna need to hire one of them scows."

I squinted in the direction he indicated and only then did I see the group of low-in-the-water wooden vessels heading our way. They barely seemed seaworthy compared to our huge steamship but very quickly nearly every passenger was jockeying for a place on the port side, waving to get noticed by the men rowing the scows. All the pushing and shoving got the captain's attention and he barked out orders for his crew: "Maintain order! Scows are rented in order of passenger class. First class ticket holders disembark first!"

The crew members were very skilled at maintaining order and they seemed to know that Silas and I were destined to be at the back of the pack, but we were both so excited to finally be in sight of our destination that we just stood out of the way and stared at the majestic scenery surrounding us.

"Dang if we didn't do it Henry!" Silas gushed. "You and me, gold rushers!" His smile was shining, "This is a momentous day in our soon-to-be momentous lives!"

His enthusiasm was catching, "Yep, today is a feather in our cap day, that's for sure," I laughed and pushed his ridiculous hat down over his eyes.

One benefit of being nearly the last to unload, we watched and learned from the others. Lowering the crates onto the scows took muscle, grunting and quite a bit of rope. The scows slowly were rowed toward shore and when they ran aground men had to slog the final thirty yards or so on foot using their snow sleds as mud sleds. The sleds didn't work quite as well in the rock-strewn mudflats but they did the trick. Anxious gold seekers pulled with all their might, eager as we were to make final landfall.

It seemed like forever, but at last it was our turn to begin the unloading process. Accustomed to hefting beer kegs at *The Lucky Break*, Silas did most of the heavy lifting. I managed to move our supplies toward the side of the ship while Silas rode to the shore and transferred it all to a growing pyramid on the rocky beachfront. Load upon load was transferred and soon a big muddy pile of our grubstake appeared on the shore. When the last load was aboard the scow, I lowered myself down into the smaller boat for my ride to land. I was so full of anticipation and I could see Silas beaming as he waved his hat in triumph. The scow bottomed out and I stood up ready to take my first step onto Alaskan soil. I gave a wave back and put one hand on the side to steady my vault over.

Silas saw me flop down and heard my wild howl. I lay there instantly helpless as the muddy sludge of Skaguay Bay seeped into my pants and boots. I began to shiver as the pain intensified. I saw my leg was bent in a very unnatural way but the only thing I could think was, 'Congratulations, Henry, you are officially the first Klondike gold rusher to fail even before setting foot in Alaska.'

CHAPTER 12

"Whoa, Henry, what happened?" Silas hollered from the shore.

"My leg is broken!" I yelled out. "Help me!" With all the speed he could muster he slogged his way out to me.

"Oh, Henry, that doesn't look so good," Silas said as he knelt down beside me, "I'll go get some of the others to help."

He turned and plowed back through mud towards the beach. He was a few feet from dry land when a huge gust of wind whipped across the bay. It must have caught Silas' hat at just the right angle because it took flight like a yellow sea gull, soared for several seconds, then plopped into the shallow water. I could see it floating for a second or two but then it disappeared.

Silas didn't even have time to react before his hat was gone. He stood still for just a moment, his shoulders slumped, and continued on, bare-headed, shouting for help from the closest group of men.

He enlisted a couple of our traveling companions: one a broad-shouldered ox of a man and the other so thin that he looked like a stiff breeze might carry him away just as easily as it had Silas' hat. They splashed out to where I lay in the mud. The skinny man was carrying a burlap sack.

"Don't worry, mate, we'll give you a hand to shore," said the larger of the two volunteers. He and Silas locked arms to make a kind of human chair. The other man did his best to slide the burlap sack gently under my leg to keep it from moving too much.

On the count of three, they hoisted me up. I'm not sure whether my yelping was louder than their grunting but we all finally made it to drier ground and my kindly mules set me down by our pile of supplies.

"Much obliged fellows, we owe you one. But don't try to collect for a while, as he's going to be pretty dumfungled for a spell," Silas said to their retreating backs.

Silas turned back to me and assessed the situation, "Dang, Henry, you are messed up. How you gonna get over the pass with a bum leg?"

I was a little short on answers right at that moment. I panted out, "I'm sorry, Silas, I just don't know."

Silas quickly shifted boxes onto the supply pile and used both of our heavy coats and three woolen blankets to make a nest on the sled for me. With his help I was able to lift myself onto the makeshift bed. He covered me up with a tarpaulin and that was the last thing I recalled until I opened my eyes onto the fresh construction lining the main road.

"Hey there Henry, glad you got a little shut eye," Silas said. "It probably was better not to be wide awake while I was hauling you up from the beach. Dang, would you look at that? Who knew there'd be so many people here?"

From my viewpoint the only open spaces to be had were quickly being grabbed up as hundreds of men and boys were pitching tents and setting up camp. Everyone was busy staking out a piece of dirt for a temporary home. Since our entire ship was loaded heavy with men and supplies on the way up, I thought Skaguay would be crowded but obviously our ship wasn't the only one to have made it here. It was a crazy boomtown.

"Yep, there's an anthill of people for sure," I agreed and tried shifting my leg into a less painful position. It wasn't possible.

"Well now, I gotta tell you I had to spend some of our money," Silas looked rather sheepish, "it just couldn't be helped but we will make it back right quick."

"What did you have to do?"

"There's still a lot of people down on the beach area and well, I didn't want any of 'em to steal our supplies. I knew I had to leave them to get you fixed up so I spent some hard cash and hired the fellow from the scow who rowed us in to watch it all until I could get back. I said I'd be an hour and I'm not sure he's any more reliable than any other so I'd best be finding you that doctor. You wait here." Silas started running up the street and I promised I wouldn't move until he returned.

Fortunately it was a sunny day and especially in my mud soaked condition I could appreciate the warmth. Lying there, I thought about my future. From the highest of hopes, I found myself nearly without any prospects in a matter of moments. What could I do now that I was crippled? Our gold-grabbing plans would have to be carried out by Silas, and I would be left alone without any chance of finding work until I could get around better. I must have dozed off again because I didn't see Silas return. He shook my shoulder.

"Henry, Henry, wake up, the doc is here."

I opened my eyes and saw a short man in a rumpled jacket leaning over me poking at my leg.

"Yep, you've got what looks to be a simple tibial shaft fracture, son. It'll need some bracing up and a layer of plaster to keep it steady while she heals," he said in a brisk manner.

"Come on, let's get the patient into my tent. It's right over there next to Jack's Tavern," he said to Silas as both grabbed the tow rope and started the sled moving. The trip was another exercise in agony and while people on the street cleared a path for us they didn't bother to give any other assistance.

I must admit this was not the triumphant entrance I had anticipated while rocking and rolling on the sea voyage up. I was now just another pile of cargo being hauled down the street with little fanfare. Braying mules hardly sound like trumpets.

CHAPTER 13

The doc's tent had two cots in it and a variety of medical equipment arranged on a wooden bench by the back wall. I wasn't his only patient—the other bed was occupied by a haggard man with a bandage over one eye. Squinting with his good eye, the man tracked my progress to the neighboring cot.

"Relax, Snuffy, you're doing alright," said the doctor as he and Silas lowered me down gently. "This here's your new roommate. What's your name fellow?"

"I'm Henry Dunhill, just arrived from Seattle on the Klickitat this morning," I replied.

Snuffy let out a rough, phlegmy laugh which soon turned into a lung-rattling hack. Between his laughing and coughing I wondered if he might expire right there but, alas, no. His guffaws continued until he fell back, nearly exhausted.

"Hey old timer, what's so dang funny?" I grunted as the doc started to examine my leg more closely.

"Yeah," chimed in Silas, "what's so dang funny?"

Both the doctor and Snuffy exchanged a look and Snuffy finally said, "Lordy, another tenderfoot within our ranks and this one really *has* a tender foot! You don't have a clue what it means to live and work in this here territory. You got your new oiled boots and your fancy jackets and you think you're going to survive life in the Klondike? What's so funny? You hardly even survived the landing."

Snuffy started to chuckle again and even though I was in pain and embarrassed, I couldn't much disagree with his assessment.

"Ah shut up, Snuffy, everyone's got to take a chance sometime. We were all newcomers here once if you'll recall," said the doc.

With authority he took a pair of shears to the leg of my pants so he could continue his examination. With the most expensive pair of pants I'd ever owned shredded on the dirt floor, the doc started eyeballing my left boot.

"Oh no sir, please, these are my only pair—'cept for the rubber boots I have back in our pile of equipment. Can't you just pull off the boot instead of cutting it?"

I realized I was setting myself up for even more pain, but I didn't really know how I could get along later with only one boot. After a goodly amount of begging, the doc conceded to my request and began the painful process of first unlacing and then tugging the boot off.

Snuffy propped himself up on his elbow to get a gander at my suffering; he may have made a few comments, but no one could've heard them over my hollering. The yanking sent a lightning bolt of pain through my leg and up the length of my spine.

"There, it's off," said the doc. "Now I've got to take a feel around to see if it needs pulling or twisting to get it back into position. Then I'll get busy fixing up a couple of support beams for you."

The doctor handed me a stick and told me to bite down on it while he worked. I suppose he wished for a little quiet and I did my best to oblige, but did it ever hurt!

As for the rest of the goings-on, I don't remember much. I'm not sure when I passed out, but upon coming to, I looked around and found that I was alone. Seemed Snuffy's injuries were of the walking wounded kind. Silas wasn't anywhere to be seen either.

CHAPTER 14

While the doctor's business might have been enhanced by being next door to a saloon, this patient had a difficult time getting any shut eye for the same reason. Tavern, saloon or pool hall, they all seem to be pretty much alike with plenty of drinking, shouting, gambling, fighting, and occasionally singing. My resting was interrupted every hour or so by a few patrons of Jack's Tavern who would 'take it outside' and commence with the verbal and physical abuses needed to settle all manner of slights and disagreements.

I hoped I would not hear Silas' voice among the crowds because we really didn't need any more complications. Fortunately, he came bursting through the tent flap about two hours later although I couldn't really tell the time anymore.

"Hey, ho, Henry, how ya doin'?" he asked as he flopped down on Snuffy's old cot.

"Silas, how are you doing? More importantly, what have you been doing? Did you get a place staked out for our camp?"

"Oh for sure, for sure. It took some doing but I got us a set up at the end of this main street. I lashed all our supplies together, snugged 'em under a tarp and while I was coming back here I decided to see about getting us some hot food. Henry, Henry, you just gotta get up and go over to Jack's; there's fellows in there that have made it rich! Rich I tell you! And they were buying drinks for everyone!"

Obviously Silas had taken advantage of the free drinks.

"I'm glad you were able to partake of such goodwill." I didn't see any food. "Did you happen to hear where these rich men actually made it rich? Did they tell you where they staked claims? What creeks did they work?"

"Oh, no, Henry, they weren't sharing any details, but I did learn they needed able bodies to help haul supplies over the Chilkoot Pass and guess what?"

I would have guessed but Silas was on a roll and didn't pause for my thoughts.

"I volunteered right then and there!" Silas' face was glowing. "They said I looked like a winner and all I needed was a grubstake of my own and I would be a 'valued member' of their next expedition! That's great, isn't it, Henry? I think it's great ..."

"Yep, that is great ... for you Silas, but what am I going to do? I'm stuck here in Skaguay until this dang leg heals up."

"Oh, yeah, I know, Henry, you're going to be okay; I made a deal with those guys and they said they'd give you a job too! It's all going to be great!"

Yeah, great, I thought. What job could I do with one leg stuck stiff as an icicle and just about as useful? While I could appreciate my friend's enthusiasm for his upcoming adventure, I was having difficulty seeing my role in any of it. Silas leaned over towards me and, in a conspiratorial whisper, assured me once again that it was going to be great!

CHAPTER 15

The next morning the doctor came in carrying a jug of water, some towels and a plateful of breakfast. "Howdy, Henry. Thought you'd need something in your stomach," he said.

I was mighty thankful to see food as I hadn't eaten anything for about fourteen hours. There was fatback bacon, a hunk of crusty bread slathered with molasses, and some steaming beans. The water was icy cold and I guzzled it down.

"Truly, Doc, you're a lifesaver!" I mumbled through a mouthful of delicious warm bread.

"Well, now, I suppose that's the literal truth," the doc laughed. "What about your friend here? Does he need some 'life saving'?" he said pointing to the snoring Silas.

"Nope, thanks. Silas got a little too much 'medicine' last night, and I doubt he's ready for any breakfast just yet," I laughed. "Thanks for loaning him a cot, though. I appreciated the company."

"Oh, don't mention it. Nobody needed it last night, so he's welcome to it."

"Well I thank you for all your help, Doc. Just let me know what I'll be owing you, and my friend and I will get out of your way," I said as I tried to sit myself up.

"Hold on there, fellow, this leg still needs some tending so you'd best stay put."

I knew the doc was right in his diagnosis; my leg was aching plenty, and I really couldn't imagine having to do much moving about.

I was startled when the tent flap snapped open and two rough looking characters came stomping in.

"Doc, got a minute to pull this splinter out of my idiot brother here?" asked the taller of the two. Both were covered in dirt.

"So, Matthew Guthrie, that's a fine splinter you've got there. How did that happen, son?" the doc inquired as he poured some water over the younger man's dirty hand to clear off the grime. He reached for a large pair of pliers and a towel.

I've had a splinter or two in my day, but to call the hunk of wood sticking out of this patient's palm a splinter –when it should have rightly been called an arrow or a lance – wasn't very accurate. I stared and shivered a little and felt my leg throbbing. What in the world?

"Damn, Doc, I was just limbing branches from a doug fir while Howard and Arnie was bucking the trunk down a ways when the whole thing started to roll. I tried to stop it from squashing me, but I guess I shouldn't have used my hand."

This fellow was speaking words I had not heard before.

"Them two used a coupla peaveys to stop the roll and came running over to dig me out of the mud," Matthew continued. "By that time, my hand was speared, so Howard sawed off what he could from the tree and then brung me to you. I guess I came out on top; I could've been pancaked right there."

I was having a hard time seeing how his 'splinter' was a good thing, but compared to being buried in the mud under a giant tree, I could imagine how a man might choose a splinter.

"Yep, Doc, he's a lucky one," said Howard, the larger man of the two. "We've been thinking of calling him just that from now on."

"Okay, Lucky," the doc said, "I'm going to pull this Alaskan-sized splinter out with these pliers and douse the wound with some grain alcohol. That part is going to hurt a bit. Then I'll stitch up the hole. You're going to have to keep your bandages clean until that puncture heals or the infection will cost you a hand."

"Yank away, Doc, it's got to be done," said Matthew as he grabbed his brother's arm for support. "I'll get me a larger pair of gloves to protect it when we're done here. Promise."

During this procedure the only person not totally transfixed by it all was Silas. I wished I could've slept through the tree surgery as well, but so far most of my wishes were going unfulfilled.

No one's going to call me 'lucky.'

CHAPTER 16

The splinter extraction was quick but did not sound in any way painless. The younger Guthrie gave a goodly howl when the doc poured on the alcohol and believe it or not, Silas finally stirred.

"What the blazes is going on, where am I?" my bleary-eyed friend yipped.

"Welcome back," I said as Silas rubbed a hand over his face. "We're in the doc's tent. You've been sleeping off last night's meetings."

"Oh, yeah, now I remember. Let me tell you, Henry, they've got some powerful drinks over at that saloon. I guess I just had one too many."

The doc had stitched up the bloody palm and declared his patient truly lucky as the splinter didn't mess with any of the important stuff inside, he could move all his fingers and probably would be back on the job soon.

"What's wrong with you fellows? You get beat up?" asked the big man as he unsheathed a giant knife, a California toothpick if ever I'd seen one.

Surely he wouldn't harm us right here in front of witnesses! But instead of menacing us, he began to pick at his fingernails—very delicately I thought for a lumberjack of his size.

"Well, in a way," I began, "I broke my leg jumping out of a scow

47

when we arrived yesterday. And Silas here just got 'too tired' to stand last night."

The big man bellowed a laugh that surely was heard in the saloon next door.

"That's the dumbest thing I've heard today," he said. "And that includes what Lucky over there did."

"Yep. You are right," I admitted. "Our first twenty-four hours in Skaguay haven't been worth writing home about."

"Apologies, let me introduce ourselves. I'm Howard Guthrie and that boy there is my brother, Matthew. We're working a stand of timber across the river. We sell the lumber to all you crazed gold seekers and also to the townies who are building stores, hotels and the like."

"That sounds like a booming business," I ventured. "How long have you been at it?"

"The Guthrie family has been in these parts for a long time—me and Lucky was born right over yonder. Our pa was also a lumberman. He saw the Alaska forests as his idea of gold and he was right."

By this time Matthew's hand was all wrapped up and the doc was folding his patient a sling of sorts.

"Now don't be foolish Matthew, make sure you keep this bandage dry and clean. Come back in two days so I can check it out, won't you?" Doc said as he finished tying the knot to snug up the sling.

"Surely will, I don't want to lose a hand or even a finger," Matthew agreed.

"Let's git, boy," said Howard. "We'll go over to Abramson's Dry Goods to get you a new pair of gloves. Thanks Doc, we'll settle up when we come back in two days." The two men pushed through the tent flap.

"They seem like nice fellows," mumbled Silas as he tried to hoist his carcass off the cot. "Ow, my head hurts something fierce."

I tried to have sympathy for my friend but by the end of the day he'd be right as rain, and I'd still be out of sorts.

"Yessir," the doc said, "those brothers are hard-workin' as you'd ever want to see. I've always been able to count on the Guthries in a pinch. Can't say that about most folks these days. If you're gonna survive for long in these parts you'd best not mistake a wolf for a dog."

CHAPTER 17

When I was finally cleared to move around, I was shocked at how weak I'd become. But—with considerable help from Silas and a rickety crutch the doc gave me—we ventured out into the sunshine. Slowly Silas and I made our way to the boardwalk that ran along the narrow street in front of Jack's Tavern. Besides setting up our new campsite, Silas had also done some reconnaissance work figuring out the lay of the land. He steered me left onto a much wider street teeming with activity.

"This hubbub is called Broadway," Silas announced. "Most everything is here and if you look up a ways you can see a joint called Denali Tavern."

Every building looked much the same to me, many still just being built. Broadway was the main street for sure. There were many freshly finished storefronts offering all manner of goods and services. The pounding sounds of hammer on nail made it clear Skaguay was hustling to keep pace with the needs of gold seekers.

"It seems to be open all day and night so that's convenient if a fellow's got a thirst."

"I'd think you'd have had your fill of the hoochinoo for a spell," I said.

"That's the truth, Henry. Too much of the stuff made a mess outta me that's for dang sure. I'm gonna stick to thirst-quenching with a cool beer from now on," Silas said nodding his head slowly.

"Nick would be mighty disappointed in me drinking the hard stuff. Now I get what he's been preaching to me all this time—a person cannot see very clearly through the bottom of a tiny glass."

The Denali was full up with drinkers by the time we hobbled by it even though it was still morning.

"Maybe later we can stop in for a cool one, "I said, but Silas wasn't listening. He pointed across the street to a large two-story building with a colorful hand-lettered sign reading Ida's Boarding House.

"Everyone I talked to said that's the place to get a good hot meal," he said.

"Noted, so let's stop in there as well when we're done with our tour."

Slowly, we passed a telegraph office and Abramson's Dry Goods where I hoped I would be able to replace my recently destroyed pants.

"On that next block," Silas said pointing to his right "is Boswell's Hardware where a person can get last minute necessities for the trip over the pass, but I think we've got plenty of supplies. Maybe we could use a can of baking powder but that's about it. We are set to go!"

Silas noticing that I was struggling to keep up asked, "Henry, you managing okay? You need a rest?"

"Yeah, I could sit for a spell. It's gonna be slow going until I get used to walking around with this crutch."

We spied a makeshift bench in front of a store called The Elixir Emporium. The front window was jammed with medicine bottles and when the sunlight hit they danced and sparkled in a prism of colors.

Silas said, "I was talking with a fellow in Jack's that first night and he's going over the Chilkoot Pass because it's a shorter, quicker route than White Pass. They call the final climb over the top the Golden Stairs—more than 1500 steps, almost straight up, all entirely in ice and snow. If we've got the right equipment, do you think that's how we ought to go over?"

"Well, there's not much 'we' in either journey, Silas. I obviously can't go with you for a good while. I suppose you'll need to hook up with some group, at least for the time being, until I can come join you."

A look of disappointment formed on my friend's face. Surely he hadn't just realized this fact. "Oh, right, right, Henry. I'm just so used to us being a team and all."

As we sat there, each wrestling with our new realities two mangy dogs trotted up. I drew back at the appearance of the animals but Silas smiled and welcomed them.

"Look here, we're already making friends," he said, as he tousled fur and gave out scratches. With a halfhearted smile to make myself seem more dog-friendly, I offered a hand for sniffing, but mostly I was just worried that these new 'friends' might have extra fleas to share. Of course, the dogs knew I wasn't really the main man in our duo. Everyone says animals can smell fear, so they continued to worm and wag around Silas, ignoring me completely.

The dogs were joyfully licking Silas' face when a loud crack made all of us jump. The brief friendship ended … the dogs turned tail and disappeared.

CHAPTER 18

"Well boys, look what we got here. I don't know if I've ever seen such sorry sacks of manure as these two cheechakos—one with a stick for a leg and the other looking about as stupid as a donkey," snarled a man dressed all in black. He rewound his bullwhip and pointed its coiled evil right at us like a snake ready to strike. The posse standing behind him started to laugh as I struggled to keep myself upright. I could feel Silas' hand shaking as he steadied me.

"Shall we introduce ourselves?" the leader said with a tone of malice.

"My name is Henry and this is Silas. We just recently arrived from Seattle," I said with a boldness I didn't feel.

"Oh, did you now? You boys going to strike it rich?" he laughed and spit, some of it hitting my plastered leg. His mouth was fixed in a cold, lifeless smile.

"Didn't I see you in Denali Tavern two days ago?" he asked, suddenly staring hard at Silas. "Ain't you the person who broke my door?"

"Sorry mister, but I don't recall breaking your door," Silas stammered.

"He's the one, Soapy, he's the one who smashed up the door when we was tossing him out," chimed in one of the gang. "I distinctly recall seeing that belt buckle he's wearing as he was leaving the saloon … in an aerial manner, shall we say." They all laughed.

"I'm sorry, sir, if I've damaged something of yours," Silas hastily apologized.

"Well now, Silas is it? I'm Soapy Smith and Skaguay is my town. These are my friends and I think I'd like it if you were my friend too. You just pay me $200 in gold to cover the cost of a new saloon door and we'll call it even." Soapy put his hand on Silas' shoulder in a manner that didn't seem very friendly at all.

"I'm sorry, sir, but I don't have that kind of money and we haven't had a chance to get any gold," Silas' voice was shaking.

"Strangle me a toad if that's not a crying shame, Silas. I was hoping we could settle up right now. But since you ain't got the money or the nuggets, it would seem that you're beholden to me, wouldn't it? No money to pay and nothing I want in trade from your measly grubstake. So how are we going to settle this problem?" Soapy asked with a snarl as his gang members moved towards us with fists clenched.

"Shoot 'em?" one of the crew suggested.

"Nah, Ed, I'd never shoot a one-legged man," Soapy said. "Now this two-legged man, that's another story."

"Oh, no, sir, please …" Silas croaked as he put up both of his hands, "no, I'll get you the money for your door…."

"That's right you will. But you said you didn't have it so how are you going to pay up?" Soapy asked. "Wait a minute. Hey Slim, wasn't I just looking for another mule to ferry supplies over the Chilkoot?"

"That's right, boss. Me and Ed are off on a very important business trip tomorrow early. We could use a strong packer such as this one here," Slim slapped my friend hard on the back.

"That's a fine idea! What if you was that mule, Silas, and I took the cost of the door out of your wages?" Soapy said.

Soapy's suggestion struck me as one that had been thought out long before being proposed. In fact, I doubted there'd even been any door damage. More likely, Silas had just been tagged as this man's latest greenhorn mark. My friend looked to me for a solution, but I was preoccupied with the menacing movement of the men toward their sidearms.

Turning back toward our tormentor, but with his eyes fixed on the ground Silas said meekly, "Whatever I need to do to pay off my debt, sir."

Soapy smiled broadly. "Now that's the right attitude, Silas my boy." With narrowed eyes, Soapy cocked his head in my direction.

"Henry, I recognize that your friend's departure may put you in a bit of a predicament given your limited mobility. Generous fellow that I am, I'd like to help you out. I've got an interest in that boarding house you saw on your walk. A fine woman named Ida runs the place and she'll see that you are well cared for while you're on the mend. Then, when you are back on two feet, you can also be in my employ."

"Nice of you to offer, Mr. Smith, but we've already got a camp set up not far from here," I said. "There are plenty of supplies in our grubstake to keep me going while my leg heals. Then I'll set off over the pass like Silas and I originally planned."

Soapy's face clouded. "If you was back in Seattle, your stubbornness just might be a commendable quality. Independent spirit and all that. But up in Alaska a man who won't accept help is just a damned fool and won't last long." He dismissed me and addressed Silas.

"Silas, my men will fetch you tomorrow bright and early. And Henry, I'm sorry that you've decided to decline my generous offer. If anything should happen to change your mind, you just let me know."

Soapy Smith tapped his bullwhip on my plastered leg and I was thankful again for Silas having hold of me. The group turned and headed down the street which by this time was cleared of people. It would seem that everyone had somewhere else to be right at that moment. Both of us wished we were among them.

"Dang, Henry, that man is a scary so-and-so, don't you think?" Silas asked in a whisper.

"Agreed, friend. He and his posse seem to have their way in this town. I wonder, is there any law enforcement around?"

"None to speak of," interjected a slight man wearing a bowler hat and an apron. He was loading a green pushcart with some of the colorful glass bottles from the display in the store window behind us. "We've got a spineless weasel who carries a badge and collects a government paycheck but he makes himself pretty scarce 'round here. Them that you just met is the ones what run this town. There ain't too many people who'll stand up to them, me included."

"And you are?" I asked.

"Howdy, I'm Hiram Addleson, your purveyor of healing tonics, balms, and the like," he said, gesturing toward the Elixir Emporium sign.

We shook hands with the diminutive man and introduced ourselves.

"So it's not just us who thinks he's scary …?" Silas asked.

"Oh, no. Soapy Smith is not a man you'd want as an enemy. But I wouldn't say he's all bad. He's downright charitable when he wants to be. Gives generously to widows and orphans," Addleson said. Tapping on a locked metal box nestled between the handles of his cart, he looked at us, eyebrows raised.

Surmising his meaning, both Silas and I shrugged—we were barely in a position to help ourselves, much less donate to widows and orphans.

"Mr. Dunhill, you look like a man who could benefit from some of my wares. I'm thinking a touch of mandrake tonic might be just the thing to ease the pain of that broken leg."

"Thank you, Mr. Addleson. That's good information, but I don't have any money to spare."

"Oh, goodness, that's fine," the tiny man said. "You know where to find me." He wrestled his pushcart back into the store and shut the door.

In silence, Silas and I moved on toward our campsite. Then he turned to me and said, "I'm worried, Henry. Things don't seem to be going the way we planned and it doesn't appear they'll be getting better anytime soon. I've got a bad feeling in my bones."

"Same here," I said. "And I doubt that elixir place sells anything that will help."

CHAPTER 19

Ve were getting settled for the night, my first night in our ten, when Silas said, "I think this could turn out okay, Henry."

Sometimes friends tell each other the truth. Sometimes friends tell the lies that they need to hear to get through the night. Identifying this as the latter scenario, I said "I think you're right, Silas. I mean, Soapy's gang might not be the most civilized lot, but I'll bet they're better suited to see you safely over the pass than I am."

"That's probably true, Henry. And while you heal up I'll get my debt to Soapy paid off. Then I'll get busy staking a claim for when you make it over the pass to join me. Soon we'll be back on track – a couple of Seattle boys striking it rich in the Klondike."

"Sure thing, Silas. That'll be great."

It was a long night; both of us grappling with our thoughts. When I'd suggested to my friend that he latch on to another group of prospectors headed over the pass earlier, I hadn't envisioned him in such sordid company the likes of Soapy's men. I could not fathom how a one-legged coward like myself might help his friend escape what felt more like a march toward the gallows than a rush to find gold.

I'm not sure how many hours of silence passed before I finally drifted off. My dreams were even more jumbled than my conscious thoughts and I woke with a start from a nightmare. In it Silas was pinned in the snow under a felled tree as a pack of hungry wolves was closing in on him. I was shivering.

It was dawn when one of Soapy's men stuck his head in the tent and snarled, "Time to get moving to the Chilkoot, ya dim-witted fice."

I don't think Silas had been asleep as he didn't seem startled, just resigned to his fate. I heard him wrestle into his boots and crawl outside.

"Well looky here, Slim, our pack animal's got shiny new gear. I ain't never seen a pair o' boots that clean, have you?"

The other man answered, "You are right about that, Ed. Wonder where a fella could get a spankin' new pair such as those?"

Under my blanket I lay perfectly still, taking the shallowest of breaths. At a loss for how to say goodbye to my condemned friend, I just pretended to be asleep. A few seconds later I was alone in the tent listening as the crunch of footsteps in the gravel grew fainter. The sun was just peeking above the horizon, and the wolves had come for my friend.

CHAPTER 20

The morning mist was heavy and I struggled to raise myself from my cot. Silas' plight weighed on my mind. Every scenario I thought about ended badly. My Seattle optimism had disintegrated into Skaguay sorrow. I could hear the activity of my neighbors, but by the time I mustered the will to face the day most folks had headed off to other business.

I hobbled out into the chill and was immediately thankful to see that Silas had already stacked up a fire pit —all it needed was a spark. I turned to crawl back into the tent to scrounge up some matches when I noticed the fire in front of a neighboring tent was still smoldering. Thinking it would be easy enough to spark mine to life using a hot coal, I grabbed for the shovel Silas had used to dig the fire pit, used it as a makeshift crutch and wobbled my way toward the nearby smoking remains.

It wasn't until I had scooped up a few embers that I realized the error in my thinking. Oh Henry just what are you going to do now without a crutch? Too late, best get on with it, so I tried balancing on my good leg with my plastered leg just lightly touching the ground while I took aim at my target. Shaking a little I drew back for the fling.

"What on earth you doing?!" A booming voice gave me a jolt, I lost my grip on the shovel and pancaked into the gravel with a thud. From the corner of my eye I saw a tall slender man, arms crossed in front of his chest looking down at me.

I stammered, "I'm sorry … I was j-j-j-just …"

"Just what?" he prompted, tilting his head and raising one eyebrow.

"Just taking some coals to try to get my fire started," I said.

He nodded, picked my shovel up from the ground and extended a hand to me. "Henry," he said.

"How do you know my name?" I asked warily.

"I don't know your name. I know my name. And it's Henry; though most folks do call me Hank."

I grasped his hand and he hoisted me to an upright position, then handed me my shovel. "If your name is also Henry," he said, "you must be the friend Silas was telling us about the other night."

"You met Silas?"

"Oh, sure. Most folks setting up tents around here are the sort that make ya wanna sleep with one eye open. A friendly fella like him is a welcome change of pace," he said smiling.

"You're right about that," I chuckled. "Silas is never a stranger anywhere for long."

"He told us you was pretty messed up and from the looks of you, he wasn't lying. Where's Silas at anyway?"

"He's gone," I said, suddenly feeling glum. "A couple men from Soapy's gang came by and …" I suddenly found myself getting choked up.

Hank put a hand on my shoulder. "How 'bout I help you get that fire going and you can tell me all about it while we cook up some victuals?"

"I'd sure appreciate it, Hank."

"If it's all the same to you though," he chuckled, "I think I'll use some matches 'stead of flinging hot coals around."

Hank pulled out some matches and made quick work of lighting off the stack of kindling and logs. I rustled around in the tent and pulled out a tin of bacon and our new iron skillet. While the fire was heating up Hank retrieved a pot of coffee he'd brewed that morning and set it on the wire grill Silas also had been thoughtful enough to position. The two of us sat down on a half-rotted log and warmed ourselves by the campfire sipping coffee while the bacon sizzled.

"So what's going on with you two?" Hank asked.

I told him that Silas had more or less been taken captive by Soapy's men and I explained how we had first run afoul of Soapy Smith. Hank hadn't heard of Soapy and I told him I wished I hadn't either.

Hank had a kind manner that set me at ease as I explained that I was now essentially alone and hopeless. He was from Canada and had made a solo trek to Skaguay in search of the same riches as the rest of us. But Hank wasn't as clueless about what he was getting into as Silas and I were because his father had gone to California during the gold rush of '49.

"Did he find any gold?" I asked.

"Yeah, he found lots of gold," Hank said, swatting at a cloud of very persistent mosquitoes. "Didn't get rich out of it though. Even gold seekers have expenses, it's not all free money you know. My old man wore out his back working for low profit and at the end was just as poor as when he'd started."

"Really? I'd be so mad if I did all the work and didn't end up with any of the gold."

"Yeah, I would too. But my father weren't mad. He said he didn't come away empty-handed at all, while he was in California he met my mama."

"Heyoo Hank!" someone hollered. We turned to look in the direction of the voice, a few tents north of where we sat, and saw a pudgy man in a green plaid shirt heading toward us. "Let's g-g-g-git ssss-some g-g-g-g-grub, p-p-p-pardner!"

"Sure, just a minute!!" Hank called back over his shoulder. "That's Roscoe from Tennessee. Arrived here on the same day as me. He stutters somethin' fierce, but he tells a story so good, you'd be a fool not to wait for him to finish."

Roscoe was out of breath when he reached us, his straight black hair matted to his scalp with sweat. He had a ruddy complexion and a toothy grin.

"Roscoe, this here is Henry from Seattle," said Hank. "He's the friend Silas was tellin' us all about."

"G-g-g-good to m-m-m-m-meet ya, Henry!" he said, extending a meaty paw.

"Roscoe's been all fired up since he heard there's a woman with a restaurant over on Broadway who makes an apple pie so good … what was it they said?"

Roscoe beamed. "So g-g-g-g-good it'll make you sssss—slap your m-m-m-mama."

"I'm not even sure what that means," Hank said. "But since we'll be on the trail for White Pass come daybreak tomorrow, it'd be a mistake to leave Skaguay without tasting that pie. Why don't you come with us? Roscoe's buying!"

"I appreciate it fellas, but with this leg, I'd only slow you down. Plus, I got a lot of setting up to do here. I aim to put together my camp stove, and the way things have been going for me, that could take all day."

"Suit yourself," said Hank. "And Henry … I wouldn't worry too much about your friend. Silas is bound to land on his feet wherever he goes. I'll bet you two end up in Dawson City up to your waists in gold nuggets."

As Hank and Roscoe ambled off in search of heavenly apple pie, I set to unpacking and assembling my stove. It didn't take me all day, though it would've gone much faster if Silas were with me. Without my friend life in Skaguay was going to be a lot more challenging, but I was feeling hopeful for the first time since Soapy had rendered his verdict. Silas was strong. He'd fare well on the trail and we'd be reunited soon.

CHAPTER 21

The day was going well. My early life hadn't prepared me for any kind of living off the land—or even living outside four walls for that matter—but I was eager to learn. Meeting Hank and Roscoe made me think that perhaps I might be fortunate enough to encounter more such kind souls along the way. I felt renewed hope for the future, at least my future here in town.

It was a complete shock when I was wrested from sleep by hands yanking me out of my cot. I couldn't even remember going back to take a rest. I saw the flames and smelled the smoke, so instead of fighting against my attacker, I joined in my rescue, scrambling and clawing my way out of the burning tent; grasping desperately for a handhold and kicking out with my feet to gain some traction. By the time I was out of danger, there was nothing to do but watch as flames engulfed everything Silas and I owned.

"Dang, pilgrim, what the deuce did you do?" I looked up and saw that I was being addressed by Mr. Addleson. He was covered in mud and breathing heavily. There were empty medicine bottles scattered everywhere around his overturned push cart.

"I don't know … what happened … I guess I was sleeping …." I couldn't take my eyes off the smoking pyre.

"That's exactly how I found you, sleeping like it was the middle of the night when everyone else had gone about their morning business in town. Got to say that's one hell of a way to wake up and sorry I had to be so rough but things were progressing mighty fast. Boy, it's lucky for you I was over here making the rounds with a few of my offerings … it looks as though you could use some of Perry Davis' Pain Killer right about now—your hand seems a bit singed."

He looked over to his upended cart where most of the inventory lay scattered in the dirt. "Sadly, it seems as though my one bottle of it broke and expelled all of its pain killing goodness into the ground."

Still in a daze, I scanned the sea of tents, all unharmed. Only ours was gone.

"Thanks, thanks for saving me, Mr. Addleson. I would have been a goner for sure. I was sleeping so soundly …. I hate to think what could have happened had you not been around."

"Not a problem, young fella, not a problem. I confess at first I didn't even know your tent was occupied. Good thing I heard a snore coming out of it," Addleson stood and dusted himself off. He bent down, righted his cart, and picked up what bottles could be salvaged.

"Let me help you," he said. He squatted, wrapped my good arm around his neck, and hoisted me onto my feet—or foot. "Let's get you to the doctor. That burn'll need some tending. Can you balance on your own for a second while I get my cash box?"

With a metal box tucked under one arm and me on his other, we stumbled our way toward the doctor's tent. Seeing us struggling to make our way down the street, one observer offered to lend me his rifle to balance on. Mr. Addleson didn't even give me the chance to respond before he declined the offer. "This damned fool would just shoot his foot off."

Exhausted by the time we reached the doc's tent, Mr. Addleson and I were mighty discouraged to find the good doctor was not on the premises. To my surprise, the lumberjacks, Howard and Matthew, whom Silas and I had met previously, were camped out in the tent. Matthew, the smaller of the two giants, was holding a fistful of bright red bandages against the side of his head and passing a flask back and forth with his brother.

"Say, friend, back so soon, weren't you already in here for that broken leg a few days ago?" Howard, the lumberjack who wasn't bleeding, inquired.

"Not the leg this time boys," Addleson told them. "Our friend here has gone and tried to set himself on fire." The lumberjacks exchanged looks as if trying to determine whether this far-fetched version of events might really be true. "We were hoping to find the doctor here to see if he might have another crutch and some burn salve to heal up this fella's roasted hand."

"Doc's gone down to the boarding house to tend to Ida's sister," said Howard.

"I didn't know Ida had a sister in town," Addleson replied.

"She come up to help Ida with work at the boarding house, but she took sick soon as she got here and ain't been nothing but more work for poor Ida," explained Matthew.

"An albatross," I said.

"No, I think the sister's name is Alice," Matthew corrected me as I began to wonder if his hearing was impaired by the bandages or if he had lopped off his whole ear. The amount of blood on the bandages suggested the latter was entirely possible.

"I don't know when Doc might be back. If you're in bad shape, you ought to just go on down to the boarding house to find him," said Howard.

"It's a long way back to the boarding house," I said, "and Mr. Addleson has already carried me farther than it's fair to ask of a person. I think I'll just wait here."

"I'll hear nothing of the sort," said Howard, the two-eared lumberjack.

He put the flask to his lips, tipped his head way back—I assumed to get the very last drop—and then wiped his mouth with a sleeve. "I'll be heading that way now to replenish my supply. This one," he held the flask upside down to demonstrate that it was empty, "didn't last too long as Matthew here was trying to replace all the blood he lost with my whiskey."

"Maybe if I could find something to use as a crutch I could …" I managed to get out before being cut off.

"Crutch or no crutch, no one-legged man is going to make it all the way down Broadway before being either washed away in this storm or buried neck-deep in mud. Given your luck, I assume it would be both."

I was about to protest that it was barely even raining at that point, but before I could even utter the words the sky outside the tent flap lit up with a flash of lightning and the tent shook with the thunderous rumble that followed.

Howard stood up as straight as he could manage without hitting his head, tucked the flask in his pocket and took a step over to me. He leaned his shoulder into my stomach, hoisted me like a sack of flour and stepped out of the tent into the pouring rain.

I called out a thanks to Mr. Addleson as the giant trudged the several blocks to Ida's boarding house. As foretold, the light rain had now become a deluge. The sort of downpour that—had it arrived earlier in the day— might have prevented a conflagration from destroying all my earthly belongings. Not too little, but definitely too late.

CHAPTER 22

Rain-soaked and shivering, I made my entrance into Ida's boarding house like a sack of potatoes. Whether the doctor was present or not, I instantly began to believe in the healing powers of this new place from the moment that my lumbering giant of a pack mule plopped me down in a chair by the entrance.

As my eyes were adjusting to seeing the world right side up, my nose told me that things had taken a turn for the better. The smell of fresh brewed coffee filled the room along with something sweet too. Flapjacks?

"What in blazes do we have here?" asked the short, dark-haired woman busy wiping down the table next to me.

"Blazes is right, Miss Ida, this here is Mr. Henry ... sorry sir, what is your last name?"

"Dunhill."

"This here is Mr. Henry Dunhill and he has had an accident. Is the doc around?"

The woman spent what seemed like an entire minute staring at me; then she stepped closer and sniffed me. I felt somewhat like a skunk cornered in a wood pile. I half expected her to grab for a broom and beat me with it.

"He sure is here Howard. I'll go upstairs and fetch him." She gave me another long look before she went across the room and up the staircase.

"Man, that food sure smells fine and I am powerful hungry!" Howard declared. "Think I'll go and see what's going on in the kitchen and bring us back some victuals." He took about three of his giant steps and was gone through a swinging door, leaving me alone. I also was hungry and hoped that my new friend would bring back piles of food.

I closed my eyes and prayed for eggs piled high, a hunk of fresh sourdough bread smeared with honey and a huge cup of hot coffee to wash it all down. I seemed to be having problems staying awake so I wasn't sure how long I was out.

"Say now what have you done to yourself?" Doc asked as he gently raised up my burned hand. "That looks to be a ripe ol' burn, son." He pulled out a blue jar from his doctoring bag along with a roll of bandages.

"Is that Perry Davis' Pain Killer?" I inquired.

"Ha! I'm a real doctor who uses real cures. Those patent medicines are so much hokum and alcohol. They're just as likely to kill the patient as kill the pain."

"Oh, that's what Mr. Addleson suggested I needed, but he didn't have any to sell me since his only bottle of it shattered when his pushcart tipped over. He saved my life by pulling me out of the fire. I'm thankful for his efforts but I think I'm about the unluckiest soul on this earth," I lamented. "There aren't many body parts left whole on me."

Doc laughed, "I think I'd agree with you son but you were lucky not to take any of that snakeoil at least. Pretty sure the cure is worse'n the disease. I'm just glad to be able to help you again because it is people like you who keep me working in town and not digging in the fields."

Ida returned and posted herself behind him watching the entire show. She laughed and slapped him on the back. "Oh Lordy, Doc, what with beatings, pistol whippings, drunkards, and gravity, you'll be busy until the day they nail you into your coffin."

"I suspect you are right, Ida, knock on wood."

Both of them immediately knocked on the wooden table; I felt like I should too but didn't have a free hand. The doc applied what he said was bear grease salve liberally over my blistered hand. It smelled ripe but felt cool. He finished up by wrapping the mess with an entire roll of white bandage.

"There now son, that makes another bill you owe me, although I don't rightly know what sort of work a fellow with only one working hand and one working leg is going to do to earn the money to pay me."

"Never mind that right now, Doc," said Ida. "Mr. Dunhill, you look like a man who could use a cup of coffee and a slice of pie. Will apple suit your fancy?"

Apple pie! That's what I'd smelled. "Ma'am, I can't imagine anything better right now."

CHAPTER 23

*S*ilas' face was frozen in fear. He frantically looked back and forth at the two men who were looming over him, one holding a hunting knife, the other a rifle pointed directly between his eyes.

"No, no, honest, Slim, I didn't touch anything of yours. This here is my own knife; I bought it in Seattle just before me and Henry came to Skaguay! I ain't trying to pull nothing on you two, I just wanted to cut off a plug of meat and I didn't know ..." Silas was babbling.

"Stealing is a mighty serious offense on the trail, Silas," sneered Slim, the larger of the two men. He raised his boot and pinned Silas' arm to the ground. In a flash he made a move to gut the prone man. Silas moved to fend him off with his left arm while kicking out with his legs. Slim fell backward and hit the ground hard. Silas still had his knife in hand as he scrambled back on his feet.

"Shoot him, Ed, shoot him!" hollered Slim. Ed smiled a gap-toothed grin as he raised the rifle and took dead aim. "My pleasure," he laughed.

A shot rang out with the echoes repeating off the rocky mountain cliffs.

It was so dark it took a few moments to realize where I was. The bed covers were scattered all around me and my burned hand felt like it was still on fire.

Silas! Where was he? Was he hurt? I slowly shook off the fog of dreams to realize that I didn't know the answers.

Hovering between dream and reality the boarding house sounds crept into my thoughts, creaking floorboards mostly, as the rest of the world continued on with life. I willed myself to come back from what I hoped was a horrible dream. Silas couldn't be dead I assured myself but I heard a gunshot, didn't I?

I pulled myself up using the iron headboard rails and gently lowered my bum leg onto the floor. A window with a thin ragged curtain was near enough for me to grip the ledge and pull myself standing. I was wrestling open the window in the hope fresh air would clear my mind when I heard another gunshot. Leaning out the window I could see into the alley. A full moon shining above the rooftops helped me to see movement, a man was scurrying back towards the main street in front of the boarding house. This was no dream. I heard others rouse themselves in reaction to the shot.

"Hell's fire, who's shooting what at this time of night?" one of my neighbors shouted. I heard other rumblings but wasn't able to move across my room fast enough to join those boarders who were already congregating in the hallway. When I finally yanked open my door, two scruffy men were making their way down to the dining room. Using the wall for support, I hopped my way towards the stairs and a sturdy banister allowed for a fairly easy descent into the dining room.

Ida already had one oil lamp going and was busy lighting a few others. "Where did the shot came from?" she asked.

"I think it came from the alley," I said. "I looked out my window and saw some commotion back there."

"Wait … what exactly did you see?" Ida asked.

"Well, ma'am, at first I thought I was dreaming the gunshot. But when I finally got myself awake and opened the window I saw one man making out for the street."

"Any idea who it was?" asked a man standing by the kitchen door.

"No sir, I've only been in town for less than a week so I don't know many people. The man was rather short and he looked to be limping. That's about all I saw."

Just then the door flew open and a tall man wearing a barkeep's apron, burst into the room. "Ida! Is everything okay? I was working behind the bar and heard a gunshot. Sounded like it come from over here."

"Thanks for checking on us Frank," said Ida. "We're okay. Young Mr. Dunhill was just telling us what he witnessed. Henry, this is Frank Brown. He works at Denali Tavern next door."

"Pleasure to make your acquaintance, sir," I said.

Frank asked what I'd seen, so I repeated for him what I had told the others. He then grabbed a lamp and led a group outside to investigate.

"You wait here, Mr. Dunhill," Ida said, pointing me to a chair. "We'll be right back."

CHAPTER 24

It didn't take long before the posse returned.

"I'll get the coffee started," Ida announced to the group as she went into the kitchen.

Three boarders pushed their way back into the dining room carrying a body. They gently laid it on the floor next to the doorway and stood, staring at the poor man's lifeless corpse. An obvious bullet wound in his chest continued to ooze blood. I recognized him right away—it was my elixir friend, my personal fireman, Mr. Addleson. It wasn't but twelve hours ago that he rescued me from certain death.

"Dump some sawdust down," Ida commanded from the kitchen, "to sop up the blood; otherwise I'll never get those floors clean."

One of the men grabbed the bucket from below the stairway and spread the sawdust all around the body. The assembled posse began to sit down, eyes averted from the sad sight. The clock which hung beside the kitchen door ticked loudly.

"So, we got ourselves another dead'un. What the hell is this town coming to? That's five dead this month alone!" bemoaned Ida as she spread out a bedsheet to cover over poor Mr. Addleson.

"Why the hell do you think Mr. Addleson was even in the alley at this time of night?" one of the men asked to no one in particular. "I mean, he isn't … wasn't a drinker so he wouldn't have been coming home from a saloon; he kept regular businessman's hours as far as I knowed him." The group murmured in agreement.

"And, why would anyone want to rob him? I mean, how much money could he have possibly stored in that lockbox he used for his 'widows and orphans' collection? It's a head-scratcher 'cuz he never seemed to do nothing to nobody. Why him?" another man asked.

"Maybe they was trying to grab poor Mr. Addleson, so's to strong arm him back to his store and force him to open up the cash register," another boarder chimed in.

That seemed a likely idea to the group, but why kill him I wondered? Wouldn't the crime be more likely a kidnapping rather than a killing? I didn't much care for the way my brain was working debating between one horrible crime and another.

Just then Ida turned her attention back my way. "Mr. Dunhill, are you feeling better? How's the burn? The doc gave you enough laudanum to sedate a horse last night," Ida revealed.

"My burn isn't quite as angry. Thanks for tending to me. Did you say I got a draught of laudanum? I don't remember taking that. I don't remember quite a bit, come to think about it," I admitted.

"That would be the point of taking that particular medicine. Some of the fellows were kind enough to carry you up to a room after the doc was finished with you, very ready to get some rest I'd say," Ida chuckled a little.

Sitting off by the wall where my bum leg wouldn't accidentally get bumped, I contemplated whether what I'd witnessed was true or just the continuation of some laudanum-induced dream.

"Well now boys, gather up the dearly departed and fetch him off to the cooling shed please," Ida commanded. "There's nothing more we can do to help tonight. In the morning maybe more will be revealed. Someone help Mr. Dunhill back up the stairs please."

While I was being aided with the stairs I could see Frank Brown and another man twist up the sheet to make a cocoon-shaped bundle and lift the corpse by the ends. Slowly they shuffled out the door with their cargo trying to be careful. A loud bumping sound belied their efforts. Mr. Addleson's head hit the door jamb on the way out. Rest in peace.

CHAPTER 25

Sunlight streamed through the bedroom window and warmed my face. My memories of the last night were fuzzy. Which parts had I dreamed? Which parts were real?

I made my way into the hallway outside my bedroom. From the top of the stairs I could see the pile of sawdust—stained a deep red—still on the wooden floor, and I knew that at least one of my vague recollections had really transpired.

"You trying to fall and break the other one?"

As I twisted around to see who had spoken, I did indeed almost lose my footing. With a desperate grab I managed to grasp the handrail and steady myself.

Behind me was a girl certainly no more than eighteen years old with long, dark hair pulled together with a green ribbon. The most splendid sight I had witnessed since leaving Seattle—maybe ever—stood with her hands on hips, her eyes twinkling and a playful smirk shining my way. I was thunderstruck.

"I'm Alice but most folks just know me as Ida's sister."

"Oh, oh ... I'm Henry ... but I'd heard that you were sick."

"Well, the trip up to Skaguay doesn't do any favors for one's health, that's for sure. I suspect you may be familiar with this phenomenon," she said, eyeing my bandaged hand. "Thanks to the doc and my sister, I'm feeling good for the first time since I boarded that dreadful ship. I told Ida that I'd come up here to help with the running of the boarding house, but so far I've just been an albatross."

I stared at her with slack-jawed wonder.

"An albatross is a big bird that people talk about having tied around their necks. It's used as a metaphor for the suffering another one fe …," her voice trailed off. I suppose she assumed I wasn't interested. I stood frozen, speechless.

"Well, since Ida's husband up and died, she's had to manage up here by her lonesome. She said the townspeople had been good to her, but I had a premonition that she was going to need some help."

Again, seeing no sign of comprehension on my face, Alice explained, "A premonition is a feeling about how things are gonna happen in the future."

"Right, sure," I burbled, my head bobbing a little too vigorously. "Well, I'm glad you're feeling better. Nobody knows better than me lately about being a burden. It's taken considerable charity from some folks up here just to keep me alive. In fact, you called the trip up here dreadful, but up until now the boat ride was the highlight of my experience."

"Until now?"

"Huh?"

"You said the boat was the highlight 'until now.'"

"Um …"

"Alice!! I could use a hand with breakfast down here!" Ida called from the dining room and saved me from having to explain my word choice to the comely Alice.

"Be right down!" Alice shouted back. "Henry, it was lovely to make your acquaintance. I hope you'll be staying with us for a while longer."

"Yeah, me too."

Alice darted down the steps, navigated gracefully around the sawdust pile, and disappeared through the swinging door into the kitchen.

Descending the stairs, I kept my eyes on the entrance to the kitchen, hoping the raven-haired beauty I'd just met might emerge.

When she did she was carrying a tray full of hot food to a table where four men sat, forks in hand. She set down plates which were overflowing with piles of bacon, eggs, and buttery bread.

Still only halfway down the staircase, I surveyed the dining room and once again felt that Ida's boarding house was a whole other world from the rugged frontier outside its doors. If I hadn't known better, I would've thought I was back at *The Lucky Break* in Seattle—a warm room bustling with the happy energy of regular patrons.

A dozen tables were filled with men ranging from the most grizzled prospectors to a group of dandies who seemed unlikely to have ever dirtied their hands in search of gold or anything else. The buzz of assorted conversations rose from the dining room, as did the aromas from breakfast, and awakened a powerful hunger in my belly.

Picking up my pace, I reached the bottom of the staircase and located the replacement wooden crutch that the doc had given me the night before. I hobbled my way across the dining room in pursuit of some delicious breakfast of my own. Ida came out of the kitchen with a fresh pot of coffee and smiled warmly at me as she refilled the mugs of customers at the table nearest the front door.

Her coffee pot now empty, Ida made her way over to me.

"Good morning, Mr. Dunhill. I trust you slept about as poorly as the rest of us last night?"

"I suppose so, ma'am. It's a shame that anyone would do harm to such a nice man as Mr. Addleson."

Ida's smile turned to a look of concern. "Well, Skaguay doesn't seem to discriminate between the nice and the not-so-nice when choosing who to take from this world. You stay here long enough, you'll say goodbye to more people than . . ."

Ida stopped abruptly and her gaze flicked over my shoulder toward the front door. She wasn't the only one to halt in mid-sentence. A hush fell over the dining room as patrons became alerted to something that had just shifted the mood entirely.

CHAPTER 26

From my vantage point I pivoted slowly in the direction of the entrance. Standing in the doorway was a man I'd seen once before but this time he was alone and he wore a look of rage.

Soapy Smith scanned the room until his gaze fell on the bloody sawdust pile near where he stood. Soapy looked up and furiously commanded, "EVERYBODY OUT!!!" The place emptied out quickly as all of the able-bodied customers hustled out the door careful not to look directly at Soapy. I stood up, crippled and trembling, until Alice took note of my predicament and helped me through the swinging door into the kitchen.

Cowering behind the kitchen door, I felt the door frame vibrate with the thunderous roar of an angry Soapy Smith. The wood muffled the words but I was able to pick up some of it, "Like a brother … gets killed without my saying so … gonna pay!!"

"Should we help her?" I asked Alice.

Alice cocked one eyebrow and gestured at the cast on my leg. "What exactly do you figure you're going to do to help her?"

"Well, I just …"

We could hear the menace in Soapy's voice begin to subside as Ida slowly talked him down from boiling to simmer.

Alice leaned in closer to try to make out the now faint conversation in the next room. I followed Alice's lead, repositioning my crutch to balance as I pressed my ear firmly against the door—a swinging door. I felt it give way, and fell straight through landing hard just inside the dining room.

Because I just couldn't seem to keep my bad luck to myself, my cast tripped Alice up and she came tumbling, face first, right after me. I would like to say I cushioned her fall, but her head slammed down hard against my own skull which didn't provide much cushion for either of us.

She popped back up on her feet pretty quickly looking more embarrassed than injured. I didn't move at all for a moment but when I finally did prop myself up on one elbow to try to get back upright, I was forced flat by a heavy black boot planted firmly on my back.

"We meet again," Soapy snarled.

"Yes sir, I'm Henry Dunhill."

"You're the cripple with the big goofy friend who broke my barroom door."

"Silas. Yes sir."

The bell over the front door jangled and Soapy looked over to see who was interrupting. A bearded man stood there in a barkeep's apron shifting his eyes back and forth between me and the man who was keeping me down.

"What the hell do you want Frank?"

"Sorry to bother you Soapy, but I think this is something you're really gonna want to see. Stinky Pete went out behind the saloon to answer the call of nature and found this half-buried in the mud," he said crossing over toward us.

Frank held up something that even from my position on the floor I recognized immediately. "It's the damnedest thing I ever saw. Looks like one of them pepperbox pistols, only the barrel is all torn apart like the thing exploded when it was fired."

Soapy was intrigued enough to turn his attention away from murdering me for the moment and reached to take the gun from Frank.

"Where exactly was this gun found?" asked Soapy.

"Well, that's why I was sure you'd want to know about it. We must've missed it when we were out there in the dark getting Mr. Addleson's body last night, but the gun was found real close to that spot, no further than it is from where I'm standing to Henry on the floor there. Hi Henry."

"Hi Frank," I said from my position on the floor.

Sensing that my death was no longer imminent and since Soapy's attention was now occupied, Ida and Alice helped me up and handed me my crutch. They positioned me up against the wall and then made their way over to get a closer look at the gun in question.

I suppose the natural thing would've been for me to want to check out the gun too, but I stayed right where I was. My shortcomings were many, but my eyesight was pretty sharp. I didn't need to go any closer to know that it was, in fact, the strangest gun I'd ever seen in my life. But this was not the first time I'd seen it.

The last time I'd laid eyes on this pistol, my best friend Silas was tucking it into his boot.

CHAPTER 27

"Poke me in the eye with a sharp stick if I be lying!" the dusty sourdough said to the gathered crowd at Denali Tavern. "That native woman were right on target when she done predicted about my mule coming up lame in one day hence. Damned if I ain't now a true believer."

"What woman are you blathering about, ol' timer?" asked a fellow looking awkwardly uncomfortable in a city suit. "I'd like to partake of some of her wisdom if she's that good."

"Hell's bells, mister, everyone knows the Truth-sayer; she comes into town to sell her charms and amulets that supposedly ward off the evil in the mountains. She don't talk much unless you got some coin for her. No white man can pronounce her tribal name good so we just call her Sunny," explained Frank Brown.

I made a mental note to find out more about this 'Sunny' and perhaps avail myself of a few lucky charms. Given my luck so far had been mighty poor, it couldn't hurt. Maybe an amulet or two would break my next fall at least.

"I'd like a lager, Mr. Brown, if you please. Any news about the murder of Mr. Addleson?" I propped myself up as best I could.

My question drew a few sideways glances from other bar patrons.

"Murder? Murder you say?" the city slicker croaked, "what the devil kind of place is this? Ain't there any law in this town?" He seemed rather shocked that an Alaskan frontier town wasn't quite as civilized as his former home.

"That's right, mister," said Frank wiping off a whiskey glass. "One of our business owners was shot last night, shot dead right behind this saloon. We've been asking around but no one knows nothing it seems."

"Maybe someone should ask that Sunny woman," snickered another of the bar patrons. "She's supposed to know everything." A group around the ol' timer laughed which set him off on another rant.

"Shut up! You don't know nuthin' ya ball of turd, ya."

"Settle down, boys, I'll not have any fighting in here today. Ben, play some music, would you?" Frank hollered over to a man standing by a piano. A cold beer, some music and what passed for convivial conversation, what more could a fellow want?

I'll tell you what I wanted—answers. Things just didn't add up because I knew Silas wouldn't murder anybody so I'd kept mum about the gun, not knowing who I could trust with my secret. I feared the worst for my friend. Silas' father had carried that pepperbox pistol during the Civil War. It was the only thing of value Silas had inherited from his old man, unless you consider big ears and flaming red hair to be valuable. So if Silas had gotten separated from that pistol, something had gone very wrong on the way over the Chilkoot.

Frank set a beer down in front of me and I turned away to survey the saloon. I saw the ol' timer had plopped down by himself at a table in the back corner. I took a long pull from my glass and decided to hobble over to join the old man at his table.

"Howdy, mister. I'm Henry Dunhill, and I was very interested in your story about the fortune telling woman."

"Oh, it ain't no story. She just knows stuff and—to my mind—she's been mighty accurate. I heard tell she told many a truth over the years, once she warned of an earthquake and damned if it didn't happen. Another time she told that boarding house lady that her man was gonna die and damned if he didn't up and do that very thing! I tell you, she's got the gift!"

My companion took the final pull on his whiskey and slammed the glass a little too hard on the table. "Ah, that's mighty fine, mighty fine." I wondered if he was angling for another free shot but didn't have to wonder for long as he whistled for Frank.

"Thank ya, mister Dung …?"

"Dunhill," I corrected him. "My pleasure. Tell me, have you ever been over the Chilkoot?"

"Chilkoot? I ain't been up and over to the Klondike fields 'cause I'm too damned old. But even if I was a young man you wouldn't catch me on the Chilkoot 'cause I ain't suicidal neither. Every soul on that trail is a world-class fool or has a death wish … or is a horse."

"My friend left with a group to go over the Chilkoot, and I'm afraid for him," I said.

"Is he a fool or just suicidal?"

"Actually, I think maybe he's the horse," I replied. "He got roped into hauling gear for some pretty disagreeable fellas."

"This time of year the trail's getting mighty difficult. There's mud everywhere, and then higher up there's the matter of avalanches. Someone yells 'Boo!' and suddenly you're buried under thirty feet of snow never to be heard from again. Even the natives who've traded on that route forever are afraid to go during the warm months," the old-timer shook his head.

"I heard Chilkoot was the quickest way to get to Dawson, though."

"Sure, that's what people say. Folks over in Dyea also talk about the dangers of running into Soapy's boys on the White Pass. But I say it don't matter what route you choose. If you've got a dollar, Soapy's gang will snatch it from you. A person's got a better chance of getting away from an avalanche than escaping that bunch."

"Soapy's men wouldn't need to look very far to find my friend," I said. "It's their gear he's carrying over the mountains.

CHAPTER 28

The piano player hammered out a familiar tune as bar patrons gravitated to the old upright to sing a song about a lass who had big feet. The noise in the room swelled to ever-higher levels and the old-timer cupped his ear as if he was having trouble hearing me, so I repeated myself, louder this time. "It's Soapy's men who have my friend carrying their ..."

Then for the second time that day I found myself in a room where a crowd was suddenly silenced as if someone had tossed ice water on their good time. All eyes turned to the bearded man in the wide-brimmed hat who had just walked through the door but this time Soapy Smith didn't pause to survey the scene or demand that everyone clear out. I suppose most of us in that saloon would've preferred escaping but instead we held still.

"This is the lead Doc pulled out of Hiram Addleson this morning." Soapy snarled rolling the disfigured metal ball between his fingers. "I went to the gunsmith and asked him what sort of gun could have shot something this small and he didn't have to think too long on it." Soapy straightened up, pulled something out of his coat pocket and in one swift motion slammed it down on top of the piano. "THIS damned gun!!"

All eyes turned to get a gander at the pistol. "People have been pretty tight-lipped about this shooting so right now I'm offering a $500 reward. I want the man who gunned down Addleson!"

Most everyone buzzed with excitement at the prospect of such a large amount of hard cash but I was trying very hard not to seem nervous. I thought about the gun Silas kept in his boot and realized what a fool I'd been to assume his secret was safe. Now there was an awful lot of money to motivate folks to remember what they might have seen. I didn't know who'd shot Mr. Addleson, but if Silas was still alive he wasn't ever going to be safe until someone figured out who might have used that tiny pistol to murder the elixir peddler.

At least one person wouldn't be claiming the reward. My drinking buddy had his head on the table and slept through the whole scene. It took some doing but I managed to shake him awake.

"Hey, old timer!!! I need to know … where can I find Sunny?"

CHAPTER 29

I have to admit I'd grown tired of hobbling down the rough-hewn sidewalks looking to find the Truth-sayer. I'd been looking for three days, every time hoping I would finally have success. The ol' timer said that Sunny hung out mostly along Broadway, near where the Cat-o-Nine-Tails was open for business, but was fuzzy about specific times of her arrivals and departures. I was becoming suspicious of the truthfulness of his tales because he probably existed in a permanently disordered state. Still, I needed any bit of information I could glean about my friend's whereabouts so an alleged clairvoyant Chilkat woman was worth a try.

The town was becoming more familiar to me as a result of my walks. I had made an acquaintance with the shopkeeper at Boswell's Hardware. He had been in town for a year and was happy to see Skaguay grow larger by the day with people afflicted with the gold fever. I asked him about the mysterious Sunny and he confirmed that she should be nearby but couldn't narrow down which day she would be around. I left and continued up Broadway.

"Howdy, mister, seems I've seen you around here in the last few days. You looking for something specific or just shopping our fine wares?" The questioner was perched on a rickety chair in front of what looked to be a boarding house or hotel of some sort. The hand-painted sign said Mabel's Place. He was smoking a cigar and his rifle was propped up against the wall behind him.

"Oh, well, you could say I was shopping. I heard that the Truth-sayer woman could be found around these parts. Do you know about her?"

He laughed and spit. "Yes, yes, everyone knows Sunny. You in the market for some eagle feathers for your hat or a wolf tooth necklace?"

I felt like he was poking fun at me. I laughed also trying not to sound nervous. "You got that right, sir. I'm hoping to see some of her native amulets, but I take it you are not a believer in her 'gifts'?"

He took a long draw on his cigar and blew the smoke out in near perfect rings. "Yep, that's right, I am not a believer—but many in these parts are. Things get pretty desperate come winter, and a man's got to find comfort wherever he can. Some find a home in church …." It looked as though he winked at me.

"There's truth in that, however, I haven't had the pleasure of living in the far north for long," I admitted. "An ol' timer told me about the native woman, and—since I'm not much use what with this cast and all—I thought I'd satisfy my curiosity while I investigated the town a bit."

"Well, you've come to the right place. Sunny usually shows up before a Saturday night. Lots of her customers are a little more agreeable, shall we say, after a few cold ones and since today is Saturday I'm thinking that curious nature of yours should soon be satisfied."

He laughed, I laughed and at that exact awkward pause, I glimpsed a woman shuffling along the boardwalk. She must certainly be the person I sought; her hair was jet black and plaited, she wore a multi-colored woolen blanket, and carried a large woven basket which looked to be full. She shrugged off the blanket, spread it out and sat down. I assumed she was open for business.

"Well, there you go mister. That there is Skaguay's own ray of sunshine and information, Sunny." He arose, hoisted his rifle and went into Mabel's Place, but not before flicking his cigar butt out into the muck-filled street.

CHAPTER 30

A huge yellow dog with paws the size of pie plates had joined Sunny and the two of them eyed me suspiciously. I turned and lurched down the block toward them.

"Sunny?" I cautiously inquired.

"Yah, Sunny," she replied. The dog stood mute.

"I heard tell you had some mighty powerful charms and—as you can see—I could use some good luck." I hopped closer to the blanket and reached for what looked to be an animal tail hanging from a leather strap.

"Yah, that's not good luck," Sunny said. I couldn't quite tell if she was referring to my plastered leg or the item in my bandaged hand.

"No?" I replied, quite unsure of how to proceed. "Is this for good luck?" I held up a metal circle that had beaded strings hanging.

"Yah, no."

I tried a different tack. "Nice dog, what's his name?" I accidentally made eye contact with the beast. His lip started to curl back.

"Yah, not my dog. No name to me." This conversation was going well.

"Um, Sunny, I was wondering if you could give me some information. That man over at Mabel's Place said you were full of it. I will gladly pay." I reached for my dwindling store of cash. "Would a silver dollar help?" Now I was getting somewhere. Sunny grabbed the coin and it immediately disappeared.

"Yah, no, you not lucky. You never find gold. Leave this land." So far she wasn't telling me anything I didn't already know or wish to do.

"Yes, I know I'm not lucky. Trust me, I know," I said, showing my burned hand. "What I really wish to know about is my friend. He left town, and I haven't heard from him. Can you help with that?"

"Yah, no. This beaver tooth good for luck," she stated, holding out another charm. I persisted with my questions, assuming my silver dollar afforded me slightly more information.

"Sunny, my friend's name is Silas, he is taller than me and has flaming red hair and rather prominent ears." I used my hands to fan my own ears out as a demonstration. "Have you seen him on the trail?"

"Yah, no. This white man I have never seen. Red hair is good luck."

Lord a mercy, I started to rethink this whole truth-finding expedition. Sunny just didn't seem like someone who could aid me in my quest. I didn't have much faith in the dog either.

"Well, I guess I will buy this feather, " I said, hoping to end our transaction altogether.

"Yah, eagle feather very good luck. Keep close to your head." I felt silly tucking the feather behind my ear, but Sunny seemed pretty insistent.

"Fifty cents," she said, as she held out her hand. I dropped the coins and turned to go, scolding myself for being so foolish. Three days looking for Sunny and I was just as much in the dark as when I'd begun my search.

CHAPTER 31

A thick cloud of cigar smoke hung over the dark interior of The Nome Saloon. A polished oak bar ran the entire length of one side while the opposite side featured four round tables filled with card players.

I hadn't planned on checking out the place but on the heels of my disappointing encounter with Sunny I decided I was too thirsty to make the trek back to Ida's place just yet.

Though I had no doubt things sometimes got rowdy at Denali Tavern, The Nome Saloon struck me as a place that catered more to the sort who didn't waste any time getting to the stupor stage. I hobbled my way over to the bar and signaled to a balding older man who, when he saw me started to smile. Before I could ask what was so funny, I caught sight of my reflection in the mirror behind the bar. I had a giant eagle feather stuck over my ear, a leg in a cast, a bandaged hand, and a fresh bruise over my right eye from breaking Alice's fall with my face three days before.

"Let me guess, your tribal name is 'Loses Fight With Bird,'" he said.

"That eagle would be the only thing I have not lost a fight with so far. I'll have a beer please."

"Here, hope it helps," the bartender said as he set my drink down.

I took a sip and asked him, "What's the card game everyone is playing?"

"Faro."

"Like the kings in Egypt?"

"Yeah, I guess. You never played it?"

"No. Do people often win money?"

"Sure, I see people win money all the time. I rarely see people leave with that money though." He moved over to another customer and left me alone to observe the action.

Two guys seated at one of the tables threw up their arms in unison and hollered a victory whoop. "JOHN AND ELMER WIN AGAIN!!" Walking in more of a zigzag than a straight line, the men crossed the room and leaned against the bar next to me.

"What's with the feather?" asked the taller of the two.

"I stampeded up here but so far all I've got to show for it is this lousy feather."

"That's a crying shame, mister. What's your name?"

"I'm Henry."

"Well, I'm John and this here's Elmer. We're celebrating because we've struck it rich, rich, rich!!! Anything you want from the bar on us. In fact," John threw his arm up in a big sweeping motion, "HEY EVERYBODY!!! NEXT ROUND IS ON US!!!" A murmur of approval arose from the assembled patrons.

"You fellas got rich playing cards just now?" I inquired.

"Oh, no, those winnings are only the icing on the cake. The big GOLDEN cake! Struck it rich just outside of Dawson, we did," said John.

"We got back into Skaguay this morning and soon we'll be heading home with our piles of gold," said Elmer.

"I'm happy for you fellas," I said trying to sound sincere. "My friend and I were hoping to do the same but Silas had to leave me behind when I busted my leg."

"That's some lousy luck, Henry. Did your friend Silas set off on his own? Tough to make it all the way to Dawson without some help carrying the burden," said John.

"No, he wasn't alone, though I wouldn't say he was in the best of

· company. Are you familiar with Soapy Smith? He pretty much runs this town I have learned. Silas got drafted to haul supplies over the pass for a couple of Soapy's men by the names Ed and Slim."

Both men took a long look at me. Our drinks arrived and Elmer raised up his glass, "To friendship!"

"To friendship," we responded.

CHAPTER 32

In his zeal to find the killers, Soapy had stumbled upon a winning tactic by declaring a reward. Few things light a fire under a boomtown quicker than the offer of $500 in gold, and soon amateur detectives were coming out of the saloons to do a different kind of digging.

My original testimony from the night of the murder had been retold at least a hundred times, the boarding house patrons acting like telegraph operators working hard to get the word out. By my second glass of beer at the Nome Saloon it seemed everyone in Skaguay knew that there were murderers on the loose and that Soapy was gunning for the guilty.

"Hey, Dunhill, got any more of them laudanum memories I might need to hear?" hollered one of the card players, a man I had also seen at Ida's. The rest of his table mates gave me the collective evil eye from across the saloon. "You wouldn't be holding out just so's you can claim the reward, is you?" The question hung in the air, waiting for an answer.

"No, sir, I can assure you I have relayed all I remember."

The questioner spat and hit the spittoon beside his table. I took that to be acceptance of my sincerity. Elmer and John both turned to look back at me.

"Thanks again for the drink," I said.

"Yeah, that's alright, you look like you could use a little help getting along these days. How'd that happen?" Elmer pointed to my bum leg. "That ain't no bullet wound is it?"

"Nah, I had an accident … or two. I suspect I'll be ready to join my friend in Dawson come next month." I really hoped that prediction would come true.

"For sure, you'll still be able to make it over the pass by next month and be shooting the chutes before the big freeze," John said.

"I truly hope so although I don't quite know if I'll be enough help to run the river rapids; it all depends on whether Silas can set us up with a boat or raft." The free beer was lubricating my speech a little; I told myself I probably shouldn't be so open with information.

Hearing that two of the Faro players had decided to take their discussion outside Elmer turned to me and said, "Henry, I've got a question for you."

"Sure thing, I guess free beer earns you a few answers."

"What does your friend Silas look like? Maybe we've seen him on the trail."

"Oh you'd know him if you saw him. He's a lanky fellow with hair that's been compared to a flaming rash," I chuckled at the thought. "He's not much to look at but he's a hard-working, kind soul. Both Elmer and John nodded as I went on. "Yeah, even his beard comes in like a carrot on fire."

"You don't say," John said, nodding his head in agreement. "Lemme refill that for you." He grabbed my glass. I knew I should get back to the boarding house, but things seemed quite amiable here in the Nome so I decided to stay a tad longer; Elmer and John were quite interested in me.

"So, that's my friend Silas. Like I said, you'd remember him if you'd seen him." I sipped my fresh drink.

"Henry, I wasn't planning to press my luck, but I see that there's space open at one of the Faro tables" said John. "I just have this feeling that fortune is still smiling tonight. Care to join in?"

"Fact is, I really don't know anything about Faro," I confessed.

"Well, it's a simple game really. Even an idiot could win at it. Case in point, Elmer's been winning big all night!" John laughed. Elmer's eyes narrowed as he appeared to be deciding how to respond to John's insult. He opted to take it in stride.

"I won't even argue with ya John. I'm a simple man who enjoys simple things in life. Give me whiskey, women, and song. You can keep the rest." Elmer clapped me on the shoulder and leaned on me to push himself off the barstool with a groan.

"Ha! Elmer, so far as I can tell, you've only managed the 'whiskey' part!" said John.

Elmer smiled, took a deep breath, and staggered toward the Faro table as he belted out a terribly off-key "Daisy, Daisy / Give me your answer, doooooooo. / I'm half crazy / all for the love of yoooooooou!!!"

"That's two out of three, boys!" Elmer called back over his shoulder as he took his seat at the Faro table. John downed the last of his drink, stood up, and leaned on the bar next to me.

"Whaddya say, Henry, old buddy. I bet you're a quick learner. We can show you the ropes at Faro, and you just might strike it rich without even having to cross the pass to join your friend, er, what's his name again?"

"His name is Silas—Silas Sprague."

"Right. Silas. So, are you gonna join us Henry?" John prodded.

"I'd like to, John, but I'm afraid I don't even have enough money to bet."

"You're in luck, Henry. You've just struck up a friendship with two of the richest men in Skaguay, and it would be our privilege to spot you a few bucks until your luck turns around." John picked up my crutch from the edge of the bar and handed it to me. At that point, I couldn't think of any other objections, so I took the crutch and followed John over to try my hand at Faro.

CHAPTER 33

I must confess my recollections regarding that evening in the Nome Saloon became pretty hazy at some point however I do remember proving John's card playing assertion to be true: even an idiot can win at Faro—at least this one could. Without much understanding of the game—beyond placing bets on the table for certain cards to come up as either winners or losers—Henry Dunhill's fortunes took a long overdue turn for the good. Hand after hand went my way until John and Elmer suggested we skedaddle before someone took issue with the amount of their money we had won.

We made our way onto the boardwalk where two rich-looking men and one less-poor-than-earlier-that-night man started in the direction of Ida's boarding house, Elmer in the middle and John and me on either side of him.

"Hot spit Elmer, who woulda thunk that ol' Henry here would prove to be the luckiest gambler in Alaska tonight?" asked John patting me lightly on the back.

"Can't say as I saw that coming," Elmer replied. "I suppose we may be borrowing money from Henry before long."

"I don't know about that fellas," I slurred, "but I can promise you one thing, next time we're at the Nome Saloon, your drinks are on me!" I snagged my crutch on an uneven board and started to fall into my companions. A strong hand interceded.

"I'm so sorry fellas, seems I'm even clumsy on my lucky nights," I said. John assured me it was okay but Elmer seemed to be wincing with each step.

"Geez, Elmer, you okay? Seems like you and me both are hobbling pretty bad tonight," I said.

"I'm okay, not to worry," he said.

As John opened the front door he said, "I suppose we'd be willing to take you up on that offer of drinks but it'll have to be soon. Elmer and me ship out next week."

"Evening ma'am," Elmer said, tipping his hat when he noticed Alice tidying up the dining area inside.

"Evening gentlemen," Alice replied, giving a wary look to my companions who remained just outside the doorway.

"Hey Alice! Fellas, this is Alice! Alice these are the fellas. Careful, Alice … or Elmer there will woo you with a song!" I tried to move toward the stairs but became aware of just how unsteady I was feeling.

I turned to my new friends and proclaimed, "We ought to meet at the Nome for your bon voyage celebration!"

"That'll be just fine Henry," said John as he tipped his hat to Alice and holding onto Elmer they headed back out onto Broadway.

It took a minute before I realized I was staring at Alice, who'd gone back to work straightening up the dining room chairs. When she noticed me gawking, her eyebrows raised up and she said, "Yes, Henry, what is it you are looking at?"

"Hey Alice, aren't those guys great?"

"I'm not sure I'd say that," Alice said and walked toward me. "What have you gotten into Henry?" She reached out and plucked the forgotten feather from my ear. "Get in a chicken fight?"

"That's no chicken feather, that's my lucky eagle feather!"

CHAPTER 34

Morning arrived along with a hammering in my head. The pounding started above my right eye and went clear down to the base of my skull, clearly a sign of God's Old Testament wrath for a night of overindulgence. It took a minute to separate the pounding in my head from the pounding on my door. I kept my eyes shut tight hoping the knocking would soon stop. It didn't and I heard my door creak.

"Henry? I'm coming in," I cracked open one eye just enough to see Alice peering in.

"Hey Alice," I had to clear my throat to mutter.

"I just wanted to check on you," she said.

"That's very nice of you."

"Not really," Alice said. "Ida and I had a bet as to whether you were just hungover or dead."

"Oh yeah?"

"Yes. It appears that I lost the bet but when you came in last night it seemed like a logical prediction," Alice teased.

"Sorry to disappoint you."

"Oh, I'm not disappointed. In fact, I'm so pleased that you're alive that I'm going to brew a fresh pot of coffee right now."

I managed to open both eyes and smiled at her. "Thank you. I'd say that's just what I need this morning."

Alice giggled. "Morning? Henry Dunhill, it's four in the

afternoon!"

Having made it downstairs for my breakfast only slightly before the dinner rush, I plopped down at my favorite spot, the table closest to the kitchen. The table backed up to a corner and I could prop up my crutch out of the busy traffic. I might also have chosen that particular seat because it allowed me to admire Alice as she brought trays of hot food out to eager patrons. Since I was her only patron at the moment she sat down to join me for a cup of coffee.

"So it seems you had a pretty crazy night mister," Alice said.

"That's for sure! I would say it must've been a dream, except …"

"Except that you appear to have been trampled by stampeding horses?"

"Well, that, yes. And this." I reached into my pockets, pulled out two wads of cash, and piled it on the table.

Alice's eyes grew wide. "You won all of this?"

"This isn't even the half of it. It was spilling out of my pockets when I got undressed, so I stashed most of it in a drawer upstairs. Seems I'm a real natural at some game called Faro," I boasted.

"Plus your lucky feather," she reached into the pocket of her apron, held up the feather I'd purchased from Sunny and slipped it back in.

"I felt foolish when I bought that thing off the old Truth-sayer woman, but I'd say it paid off big. Plus I met those fellas, John and Elmer. Maybe some of their luck rubbed off on me too," I said.

"Henry, you seem to be a pretty trusting person but trusting is not what a person who wants to survive in Skaguay needs to be. I haven't been here very long myself but I know that not everyone has your best interests at heart."

"What do you mean? John and Elmer? Those guys are terrific."

"I just have a feeling, that's all. When something seems too good to be true …" Alice began before I interrupted.

"What?! All the bad things that've happened to me since I got to Skaguay … those guys are the first ones to really help me out."

Alice stared at me in silence for a moment. "You don't say

Henry."

"My best friend, Silas, got pretty much kidnapped and marched off over the mountains leaving me to fend for myself," I said. "John and Elmer are good guys, Alice. Plus, why shouldn't a man have friends?"

"And why shouldn't a village have an idiot?" Alice said.

It's difficult to angrily storm out of a room with a leg in a cast, but I'd heard enough. I hoisted myself up on my crutch and headed for the front door of the boarding house.

"Hey, Henry! Now that you've got money and someone has FINALLY helped you, maybe you could use some of that money to pay my sister for putting you up here!" she called out before storming through the kitchen door. Alice's angry exit was a lot more dignified than mine, but I managed to fumble my way out the door and stood in front of the boarding house wondering what the devil I was going to do next.

Not wanting Alice to come back out and see me looking lost, I decided to set off in the direction of the Nome Saloon.

CHAPTER 35

In spite of my anger I was struck by how pleasant the weather was. The sun was setting over the buildings to my left and a warm, gentle breeze swept the unsavory aromas of Skaguay off to some less fortunate location downwind. I saw my lumberjack friends Howard and Matthew Guthrie walking along the opposite side of Broadway. They both waved as they passed, I waved back, getting a clear view of Matthew's now unbandaged ear. It appeared that he had not cut off the ear entirely, but what remained was such a scarred and mangled mess that I wondered if that was actually a preferred outcome.

The street outside Ida's seemed pretty empty compared to most evenings. I viewed this as a good thing as it allowed me to move along with greater ease. I did wonder though, where all the people who would normally be heading to some Skaguay establishment for dinner had gone. I didn't have to wonder for long.

About a block away the boardwalk was so crowded that it spilled over into the street. As I moved closer, I could see men clustered around three horses that stood stock still in the middle of Broadway. On two of the horses sat men I recognized from my first run-in with Soapy and his gang. It didn't appear that anyone was riding the third horse which looked to be weighed down with equipment. Only when I'd maneuvered around the perimeter of the crowd was I able to get a better look. What I saw was horrific. The third horse was indeed weighed down, but it was not carrying any supplies. What I'd thought was the better part of a grubstake was actually two dead bodies draped over the saddle. From my vantage point at the edge of the crowd I could see the backs of the dead men's heads, one with long, scraggly blond hair and the other cropped short and black. Both corpses were crusted with blood. And flies.

The crowd was abuzz as those near the front relayed their observations to those who couldn't get in close enough for a peek. The men riding the first two horses sat silently, each man with his eyes fixed on a spot somewhere in the crowd. The excited voices faded to whispers and finally to hushed silence. As if pushed back by some magnetic force the crowd began to shuffle aside and I already knew what would emerge from their midst. I watched as a wide-brimmed black hat moved closer to the horses until a steely-eyed Soapy Smith appeared.

With a nod to his men Soapy stepped up to the bodies. He grabbed the hair of the blond man and lifted it as if he were going to ask the dead man a question. Many in the crowd averted their eyes not wanting to see the gruesome sight. I've heard people say that scavenging animals come for the eyes first and the mutilated face before me did not provide any evidence to the contrary. What flesh remained was a ghastly pale, a stark contrast to the deep black slit across the man's throat. I shuddered.

Soapy lowered the blond man's head and moved on to inspect the face of the other body in the same manner. After witnessing the horrible sight of the first face, most people didn't even look up to see the second one. But I did. I continued looking even though I had no doubt as to what I would see. I couldn't stop looking because there, draped over that horse were the corpses of Ed and Slim, Soapy's men who had taken my best friend over the pass.

Soapy signaled to the two men on horseback and the procession began a slow walk up Broadway and away from the crowd. Soapy stood still and the crowd remained quiet, seemingly awaiting a cue from Soapy before also taking their leave.

He raised his eyes and very slowly scanned the crowd from left to right and I focused all my attention on the ground. After a few moments I realized I wasn't breathing so I took a deep breath and chanced looking up. My eyes connected with an icy stare fixed firmly on me. I was frozen in Soapy's gaze. Suddenly he turned and headed in the direction of Ida's boarding house and the crowd began to disperse. I wanted to feel invisible and probably was to most of the people shuffling off but one person had seen me.

Anxious to get away from the scene I made a pivot to escape and saw Alice hurrying toward me. "Henry, what happened? Are you alright? You look like you've seen a ghost? Who are those dead men?"

"Those are the same men Silas left with," I whispered.

"Oh," her hand went up to her mouth, "oh, I hope … I … don't know what to say…."

She reached into her apron pocket and handed me the lucky feather. I took it by two fingers, twirled it around for a second then let it drift into the muddy street.

CHAPTER 36

Although he hadn't said a word to me, I took Soapy's dark stare as my cue to put maximum distance between us and since he was headed in the direction of the boarding house, I hobbled the opposite way. Most everybody must have been thinking along the same escape lines because a considerable gathering had formed outside the Nome Saloon. Alice had gone back to Ida's so I tried to blend into the crowd when I heard a familiar voice call out.

"You! Luck! White man red-head friend, yah?" I turned around and saw Sunny, the alleged Truth-sayer, sitting in her usual spot with the yellow dog but today was not her usual day to be in town. Since our previous encounter had left me inclined to agree with the man outside of Mabel's Place about the extent of Sunny's mystical powers I eyed her skeptically.

"Luck for you, yah?" She motioned for me to come closer.

I shook my head and said, "No thanks," and continued toward the saloon door. Her mangy dog chose that moment to move from his spot by Sunny to block my path. Sunny again motioned for me to come over.

"Red head. Luck!" she said and then put her hands behind her ears pushing them forward, "Friend, yah!" she said.

I looked at Sunny and slowly made the same gesture back at her, the way I'd done when describing Silas to her in our first encounter.

She nodded once, "Yah!"

"You've seen my friend Silas?" I asked, hobbling over to her. Her dog obliged me.

"Yah. See this man."

"Where did you see him?"

"Yah. Sheep Camp. You luck."

"Is Silas okay? The men he was with are dead. Do you know what has happened to Silas?"

"You luck!" she declared and held up something that appeared to be some sort of bone with a leather strap attached. Reaching to take the object from her she closed her fist tight around it, "You buy!"

"No, I don't want to buy anything. I just want to know where Silas is. Can you tell me?"

"Yah. Luck! You buy!" Sunny said.

"Yeah, thanks a lot but I already have a lucky feather." I turned to leave, but once again the dog was fencing me in only this time he snarled. For a dog she didn't claim, Sunny seemed to have a really good scam worked out with this giant mutt. Since I was flush with Faro winnings, I thought it better to part with some cash than to take my chances with Sunny's four-legged sales associate.

The coins disappeared and for the second time that week I departed from this woman feeling like a fool. I shoved what appeared to be a whistle into my pocket and headed toward the Nome. His work complete, the dog cleared out of my path and returned to sit by Sunny's side.

CHAPTER 37

The scene inside the Nome Saloon was considerably more boisterous than it had been on my first visit. The dramatic parading of the remains of Ed and Slim down Broadway had stirred up the masses and the noise of speculation about what had happened to Soapy's men spiraled around every corner of the place. I scanned the bar hoping that I might spot John and Elmer, a couple of friendly faces to brighten a day where all signs seemed to be pointing towards doom.

Soapy hadn't made any accusations or direct threats, but I assumed he was doing the same calculations I had done when I saw the horses: three men had left for the Chilkoot Pass, two of them were murdered. One was unaccounted for. I knew Silas was no murderer. Maybe Ed and Slim had put him in a position where he had no choice. But what could that have been? They did not appear to have been killed as the result of a struggle. Their matching fatal neck wounds were evidence of a cold-blooded execution not just a fight on the trail.

Elmer was chatting with the bartender so I made my way over to him. He greeted me warmly and cleared some room with an elbow.

"Hey Henry, looks like you're gettin' along better'n you was when we dropped you at the boarding house," he laughed.

"Still a bit of a headache, but otherwise not too bad. Where's John?"

Elmer gestured over his shoulder in the direction of one of the Faro tables. "He's over there being separated from some of his money."

"He's not so lucky tonight?"

"Nope. From what I can tell ol' John's strategy must be to lose money as fast as possible so he won't have to haul so much of it with him to California."

John looked up from his cards and saw us watching him. He jutted his chin up and gave a broad grin. I recognized one of the men seated next to John as Snuffy, the mean old coot from our first day in Skaguay. Snuffy squinted in my direction and went back to his cards.

"Sorry to hear that John's having an unlucky turn," I said, "but I'm happy you're here."

"Happy to see you too. From the reception you got from your girlfriend, me and John was worried we'd seen the last of you," Elmer smiled.

"My girlfriend?"

"Yeah, the pretty little gal at the boarding house. She seemed none too pleased when you turned up in the shape you was in with the company you was keepin'," said Elmer.

"Oh. Alice. She's not my girlfriend though I suppose you're right that she's not been too happy with me."

"Well, you'd best mind your P's and Q's, boy. A beautiful woman in Skaguay is like an albino unicorn feasting on four-leaf clovers during a blue moon," Elmer chuckled.

"Huh?"

"Rare, my boy. That's what I'm saying."

CHAPTER 38

A collective groan came from the Faro players and I watched as John pushed back from the table and walked over to join us at the bar. He slapped me on the back and signaled the bartender to bring another round.

"Hey, Henry, what do you make of all this? People been sayin' those poor fellas what turned up dead worked for Soapy Smith. Wasn't you just telling us about him last night?" John asked.

"Yeah, they were Soapy's men alright." I agreed.

"You knowed them fellas, er, knew 'em?" asked Elmer.

"Afraid so. Those two were the men who hauled my friend Silas off to cross the Chilkoot."

Elmer's eyes got big as he processed this information. "Oh, Henry, I sure hope your friend is okay. I mean … wait. You don't think …? Would Silas have killed those two guys? Sounds like he wasn't too happy to be going along with them in the first place."

"Silas wouldn't hurt anyone but I don't think Soapy knows that. And Soapy's definitely out for revenge, so I'm very worried."

I looked over my shoulder as I said this and noticed that the Faro table John had given up on had now been abandoned. Apparently, no one had brought their lucky eagle feathers.

"Well, what're you gonna do Henry?" asked John.

"What can I do? I suppose if I had two good legs, I'd already be out there looking for Silas. But it's my understanding that the golden staircase over the Chilkoot is 1500 steps straight up. I'm struggling mightily with the twelve steps just to get to my room at the boarding house."

John and Elmer exchanged a look and turned back to me. John said, "Suppose you had somebody with two good legs—or two somebodies? They could find Silas for you, bring him back safe and sound and clear this whole mess up." I couldn't believe they were proposing what it sounded like they were proposing, so I waited for more explanation.

Elmer said, "Yeah, Henry. Me and John'll go up there and your new friends will find your old friend. Whaddya say?"

"That's real generous of you to offer but you said you're taking a boat to California soon. Aren't you worried you wouldn't make it back in time?"

Both men laughed. John said, "Henry, when you've got as much gold as we do, the ship sails when we say."

"Besides," Elmer chimed in, "we don't even know how far those guys made it before … well, you know … I'm just sayin' we may not have to climb the Chilkoot. Maybe your friend Silas found hisself a woman in Dyea and decided to just sit tight until you healed up enough to join him."

"And, if that's the case," said John, "it should be easy to find Silas. A tall guy with bright red hair. No one's gonna confuse him with the natives over there."

"I suppose that's true, he's hard to miss even in the dark."

"It's settled then. John and I will set out first thing tomorrow," said Elmer.

John held up his hand. "Hold on Elmer, this is only if Henry here makes good on what he promised us."

"Ooooh, right …" nodded Elmer.

"What's that?" I asked suddenly feeling worried.

John smiled and slapped me on the back again. "The drinks Henry, you said the next time we got together the drinks were on you."

"Ah! I vaguely remember that pledge. Not a problem, I'm good for it." I dug into my pocket.

John flagged down the bartender. "Barkeep, this gentleman here is treating us tonight but only one beer 'cause Elmer and I have to get a good night's sleep. Tomorrow we're off to find the long-lost Silas of the Red Hair!"

CHAPTER 39

After my two new friends had finished their cold ones I bid them farewell and hoped they would find my friend safe and sound.

"What's that thing?" asked the bartender sweeping all my proffered coins into his palm.

"This? Oh, a whistle I think. Another ill-advised purchase from my friend Sunny," I said.

I picked it up and blew. Nothing. "Works about as well as expected," I joked and shoved it into my pocket.

"And you were the guy in here with the lucky feather," the bartender said. "Seems like that one was working just fine because you left here with a pile of winnings from the Faro table, as I recall."

"If you recall much from last night that makes one of us," I chuckled. "To nobody's surprise my luck has taken a sharp turn for the worse even since then. The feather and I have parted ways."

"Sorry to hear that pal. It looked good on ya."

Just then there was an uproar at the other end of the bar. Everyone in the saloon turned toward the commotion where a familiar face emerged from the crowd. Snuffy was standing up on a chair like he was making a proclamation.

"Pepperbox? Are you kidding me? I'll tell you who knows more than they're saying ... that man over there!" Snuffy yelled, pointing at me. "That there midget gun what killed the medicine peddler? I seen that gun in the doc's tent when I was … hurt. That gun was owned by the red-headed friend of yours!"

Snuffy leaned forward like maybe he was going to poke my eye out with his dirty finger but gravity got the better of him and he landed with a thud, face-down on the saloon floor.

The bar erupted in guffaws at Snuffy's dive but I didn't join in because now I wasn't the only one who knew about Silas' gun. Soon the whole town would know but even worse so would Soapy Smith. I limped out hoping to make it back to Ida's without being noticed.

CHAPTER 40

There isn't much that will soothe a savage hunger more than the smell of frying bacon and just the aroma made me hurry along hoping the bacon was accompanied by mounds of fluffy eggs, toasty brown biscuits, piping hot coffee, and beans slathered in sorghum. By the time I got downstairs most of the boarding house denizens had finished mopping up the remnants of their hearty breakfasts and a few were lighting up cigars. I hopped the last few feet to my usual table by the kitchen doorway and prayed the next vision before me would be a luscious steaming concoction on a big blue plate. I did have a lot weighing on my mind but for those brief moments my thoughts were filled with glorious food.

I didn't have to wait long before through the kitchen door came my vision. Alice, carrying a full plate, gave me a smile and arranged it in front of me along with a napkin, knife, and fork. For a moment, I considered having a short conversation with her but it seemed both of us had something else on our minds. She went back to the kitchen to fetch the coffee and I hunkered over my plate, vulture-like, and sucked in all the wonderful smells. I nearly choked on my first bite as I loaded the fork a might more than a mouthful.

"Slow down, Henry, that food is not going anywhere but down your gullet. You're acting like a sled dog fighting for a hunk of horse meat." This observation came from one of the fellows who had found Mr. Addleson's body behind the boarding house.

"Mmfft," I mumbled as syrup dribbled down my chin. I agreed with his observations but couldn't really verbalize at the time. The man was smiling and was just being friendly I suppose. He lit a cigar and sent the smoke upwards.

"Gotta say, there's mighty fine fixings here at Ida's. It's her food that keeps me in town, no powdered eggs here," he said. "Well, that and I already have been to Dawson twice and lost a few toes to frostbite coming and going." He laughed and I gave him my best full-mouth smile.

"So tell me, what are you thinkin' about them two who didn't make it to Dawson? I mean, frostbite's one thing, kind of expected 'round these parts as most fellows are missing a tip off something. But getting a throat slit? That's just plain butchery, wouldn't you agree?"

I stopped shoveling in food and looked at the man dead on. Ever since last night when that ol' fool Snuffy gave me the crooked finger of accusation, I had become more worried about people's motivations. Was everyone looking for my friend, Silas? I tried not to add any fuel to the fire.

"I wouldn't want to speculate, mister. I don't know anything about what might've happened to those unfortunate fellas out on the trail."

The man returned his focus to the cigar smoke and I went back to devouring my meal.

CHAPTER 41

When I finally looked up from my plate the man with the questions was gone but I couldn't spend any more time thinking about what he said because just then Alice pulled up a chair across from me.

"I'm sorry about what I said yesterday Henry. I know you've been having a tough time."

"Yeah, thanks. I wish I knew what to do to turn my luck around."

"Given up on eagle feathers, huh?"

"Yeah, but just to show how slow I am to learn a lesson, I saw that Sunny woman last night and she convinced me to buy this thing," I said and put the whistle on the table.

"Oh Henry, you must be her best customer!" Alice said picking up it. "What is it?"

"It's a whistle carved out of an animal bone, for 'good luck' I suppose but because it belongs to Henry Dunhill it doesn't work."

Alice examined it for a moment and then put it to her lips. Even knowing that had been a dud for me I half-expected it to produce beautiful music in Alice's hands. She tried it a couple of times but ultimately had the same amount of success I'd had with it.

"Strange," she said, holding it up to the light. "Wait a second … there's something stuck in here."

She reached into the pocket of her apron and pulled out a big nail. I looked at her with uncertainty trying to figure out why she was carrying some sort of dagger to serve breakfast. Seeing my concern, Alice said, "Haven't you ever seen a 16-penny nail?"

"Well, I suppose I have ... but not usually at the breakfast table," I said. "Why do you have it with you?"

"Perhaps in a town like Skaguay, a gal could find all sorts of uses for it, like to fend off an attack from a hungry wolf ... or to discourage an errant hand. Truth be told I don't usually carry it around but things aren't feeling right, you know?"

"Have pity on my poor hands," I said, "and they will mind their own business. Also, I share your feelings about things not being right." Things certainly had not been right in my world since leaving Seattle.

"See that your poor hands do stay out of any more trouble," Alice said smiling. She used the tip of the nail to dig into the whistle and surprisingly coaxed out a tiny roll of paper. Before we examined it, though, she blew into the whistle and a shrill blast startled both of us. We laughed. I picked up the piece of paper which had landed in a syrupy spot and was now a bit sticky.

"I wonder what ..." I struggled to unfold it but finally was able to read the message. Immediately my stomach flip-flopped and my heart raced.

Alice waited and finally asked, "What Henry?"

"You were right," I said in the flat voice of a man too stunned to figure out what the appropriate emotion might be.

"About what?" asked Alice.

"I am an idiot," I said as I handed her the paper:

Witnessed murders. Hiding Sheep Camp.

CHAPTER 42

"Oh my gosh Henry, your friend isn't dead!" Alice leaned in and whispered.

"It is great that he's alive but if he comes back to Skaguay right now I'm not sure how long he's gonna stay that way," my voice shook.

"What can we do to help him?" asked Alice.

"I think the only thing that's going to save Silas is proving who really killed those men and I'm the only person who hasn't already decided he's the murderer."

"You're not the only one, Henry," Alice said. "I don't think you'd be friends with someone who would murder people."

"Thanks Alice."

"Maybe we should ask ..." She was drowned out by the sound of caulk boots pounding up the boardwalk. Abruptly the clatter stopped and the door flew open. Filling up the doorway were the lumberjack brothers Howard and Matthew Guthrie panting as if they'd been running full sprint. They spotted us at the corner table.

"Henry ... we come over here to warn you ... word about the gun ... got back to ... Soapy and a whole slew of his boys are headed this way," Matthew wheezed, "and they're fixin' to find out what else you know."

"Word about what gun?" asked Alice.

"The gun that killed Addleson. Folks are saying it belonged to

Henry's friend Silas," explained Howard. Alice looked to me anticipating I would dispute the claim but I just shrugged.

"Soapy's got it in his mind that you know more than you're letting on and he says his boys will get you to talk one way or another. You gotta get out of here now!" urged Matthew.

At that moment we again heard pounding from heavy boots, lots of them this time, a stampede of boots rapidly approaching. I caught a glimpse of the mob and the guns they carried outside Ida's window right before Alice grabbed my arm and dragged me into the kitchen.

The front door was thrown open with such force the entire floor shook. I could hear shouting in the dining room as we slipped into the alley as quietly as possible.

"Henry, hurry across to the saloon and I'll go 'round front to get Mr. Brown to let you in the back door there. Hopefully you'll be safe in his big storage room until we can figure out a plan," Alice whispered and she disappeared down the alley.

Her plan seemed way better than hanging around waiting for Soapy to find me so I started my hop over to the next building. Since my crutch was still in the dining room it was slow going. I kept looking toward the street while trying to navigate the twenty feet between Ida's and the Denali Tavern but I was so focused on my mission I didn't notice I had company. I heard a noise and turned to see two men; one with a ratty brown hat and another wearing a red checkered shirt. They lunged and I tried to fend them off. I didn't get a clear look at the third man before a pistol butt connected with my head.

CHAPTER 43

I can't breathe! Struggle for air. Water rushing all around me. Water, water … cold against my face. I hear screaming. Mrrrgglllll hmmffff I shake my head to wake up, to force my eyes open. Why can't I see? A pull on the back of my head. I am hoisted up into the light. A searing pain in my lungs. I gasp for air. Through a flurry of dark spots I see a panic-stricken Alice being restrained by the red shirted man. I try to call out, the left side of my mouth feels swollen, heavy. My head snaps back. I hit the ground and fight to catch my breath.

"Where is Silas?!" the enraged face of Soapy Smith slowly came into focus.

"Alice," I blubbered getting out the word I'd been unable to before. A new pain shot through my jaw and with it the salty taste of my own blood.

"Look at me!" Soapy yelled. "Who does this gun belong to?" Soapy brandished the pepperbox pistol in front of my face. I shook my head, not as a refusal to answer but because I wanted it not to be true. Soapy glared while I received a boot to my right side from one of his men. I realized that I was in front of Ida's boarding house. Some townspeople had gathered around but I could only hear one voice.

Soapy growled, "This is the gun that killed Addleson and you know who it belongs to!"

Staring into his crazed eyes just inches from my face I reluctantly nodded.

"This is Silas' pistol," he said, "so where is he?"

"I don't know," I stammered. Another swift kick to my left side.

"I don't know where he is," I repeated trying to move my jaw as little as possible, it hurt something fierce.

"I don't believe you," he said.

"Honest, Soapy, the last I saw Silas, your men were hauling him away from our tent to do your bidding."

"And those men are dead now murdered by your friend Silas no doubt."

"Silas wouldn't hurt anybody …."

"Then how come Ed and Slim are dead and Silas is nowhere to be found?"

"I don't know who did it. I just know it wasn't Silas," I said.

"Where is Silas now?" Soapy pulled me upright.

"I really don't know, I don't."

"You haven't heard anything from him?"

From out of the corner of my eye, I spied Alice with her hand in her apron pocket.

"No, nothing," I lied, "I haven't heard from him Soapy. I would tell you if I had."

"You're a no-good liar, Henry but that's okay. My men here will administer another dose of refreshing trough water to help wet your whistle." Soapy spat as his men moved in around me. I barely had time to take a breath before two of them plunged my head back into the cold water. They held me under for another eternity before tossing me back into the mud. Another blow from a heavy boot and I was sure they'd broken some ribs.

CHAPTER 44

"**S**top it! Soapy Smith, you stop this right now!!" The voice made the same plea Alice had but this time Soapy relented and signaled to his men to stop the beating.

"Mind your own business, Ida," he snapped. I could feel his eyes still locked on me.

"I am minding my business Soapy. This boarding house is my business and I very much mind you beating a man to death in front of it," Ida fumed. "Henry didn't kill those men and you know it."

"No, but his friend did and I think he's been holding out on me."

"You know very well there are more'n two dozen people who'd want to kill your men, given the opportunity," Ida said her hands on her hips.

Soapy turned back to me and snarled, "When I find Silas, he's a dead man and if I find out that you've been lying to me you'll meet the same fate as him."

With that Soapy started to walk away but then turned back and picked up my crutch. He stood over me and his menacing scowl turned into a broad smile as he raised the crutch and brought it down hard onto my cast. A lightning bolt of pain shot straight up my spine. Soapy dropped the crutch, now broken, and walked away.

Ida and Alice rushed to help and the Guthrie brothers stepped forward from the gathered crowd and got me inside the boarding house. I was getting used to having them around whenever I needed a lift.

"Alice, you go get the doc," said Ida, "and let him know Henry's going to need to be patched up … again."

Alice hurried out while the Guthries propped me up in two chairs near the stove in the kitchen. When they had me situated about as comfortably as my condition allowed a strange feeling came over me and I began to laugh, a small laugh of amusement at first that grew into a powerful guffaw. Tears began streaming down my face. Even though my ribs ached and my head throbbed I couldn't stop. All three of them looked at me like I'd lost my mind.

"Henry, what on earth is so funny?" asked Ida.

"Well, I was just thinking, here I've been feeling guilty about Silas getting marched off to who-knows-where while I sit around safe in Skaguay. But as it turns out me trying to mind my own business is gonna get me killed faster than any hungry grizzly bear Silas might meet on the trail." The others chuckled but didn't dispute my observation. Everyone could see that Henry Dunhill was being buried under his own personal avalanche of lousy luck.

At that moment a scraping sound just outside the boarding house made us all look toward the window to see what was happening. The huge man in the red shirt had dragged a chair just outside the front door and was settling down with a rifle across his lap. I now had a guard posted to keep watch over me.

CHAPTER 45

Ida sent the Guthries on their way with leftover corn muffins and Alice fussed around trying to give me some semblance of comfort. A third chair was pushed up to elevate my legs and while the stove was warm and I was being well cared for I knew it was going to be a long night.

Both my nurses finally went upstairs to bed. Doc had given me another dose of pain medicine, but if I was to aid my friend Silas I really needed my wits about me so I only drank half of it.

Staring at the embers glowing in the cast iron stove I thought about Alice, how she had proved herself to be a loyal friend today. Even as Soapy's henchmen were using me for their cruel amusement, Alice did not betray me or Silas, a man she had never met. I vowed to tell her how grateful I was come morning. I blew out the oil lamp on the table next to me and in a few moments heard noises outside the back door. I assumed it was scavenging dogs on their rounds rummaging for food scraps. I could feel the medicine working so I decided to close my eyes and take a short nap. After a little rest I would work on my Silas problem.

I jerked awake when I felt a hand cover my mouth. I struggled to fend off another manhandling but was pinned in my chair cocoon.

"Henry … it's me … Silas. Be quiet because there's a man asleep outside the front door with a gun." He lowered his hand and even in the dark kitchen I could make out his red beard and eyebrows. He had a dog with him too. The dog sniffed me and then plopped down by the stove, panting.

"Silas!" I whispered. "Silas, I was so worried about you. Are you alright?" I could hardly believe he was here with me again.

"Henry, I have so much to tell you—"

"Wait. Not here." My mind raced over the layout of the boarding house; where could we go without being seen or heard? Leaving the kitchen would be too dangerous with Soapy's henchman snoozing by the front door. Also any of the residents could wake up, see Silas and recall the reward offer. Finally I remembered—the root cellar! I re-lit the lamp and pointed.

"Silas," I whispered, "pull up the trapdoor to the root cellar. We can go down there and talk."

Almost immediately the dog knew where this parade was going. She scratched at the trapdoor as Silas pulled it open. I lowered myself off my perch and scooted across the floor.

"What train hit you, Henry? You've got a story to tell me also I see." I was so happy to see my friend.

A cool, musty air wafted from the root cellar. Silas descended quickly and I unceremoniously thumped down the wooden stairs landing on a blanket of straw. I let out a grunt of pain. The dog prepared to jump in with us but there wasn't any available room. She wagged and whimpered for a short time then circled two times and took up sentry duty by the opening.

CHAPTER 46

Silas helped me get settled and pulled the trapdoor shut, plunging us into darkness. "Hold on, I've got some matches," I was about to strike one when he grabbed my arm.

"Henry!" Silas said, "Straw and matches don't mix—as you might imagine!"

"Oh, I'm pretty sure I can imagine alright." I wondered how to explain that within a couple hours of him leaving town I'd burned up our tent and all of our grubstake. Silas pushed the door back up and scrambled to fetch the oil lamp. I spied a small jar of peaches and handed it over to prop the door open slightly. It worked perfectly allowing in air while shielding us from the watcher.

Silas cleared out a space on the lowest shelf for the lamp and in the glow, I saw we were surrounded by sacks of potatoes; bunches of carrots; hanging salt-cured meats; jars of fruit preserves; and a couple of casks containing some form of fermenting beverage. No doubt this stash would continue to grow as Ida prepared for the harsh Alaskan winter. I also got a look at my friend and if not for the flaming red beard I would've thought him a stranger. On his head he had a broad-brimmed hat that appeared to be woven from some sort of straw. It tapered gradually upward and formed a cylinder at the top that looked like a chimney. The front featured a design of two wide-mouthed, large-eyed faces, one outlined in black, the other in red.

Silas was wrapped in a heavy woolen blanket like the kind Sunny wore. I knew she must have had a hand in outfitting him for his surreptitious journey into town. Regardless of how he looked I was so glad and relieved to see him.

"How did you even find me here, Silas?" I whispered. "When you left we still had the tent at the end of town which I stupidly burned to the ground."

"You burned up our tent?" Silas asked. "That should be a good story. But to answer your question that native woman, Sunny, was the one who helped me after everything went down on the trail. She told me there was a white man asking about me in Skaguay and she described you perfectly so I knowed it was you. She called you a crippled crow. By the way did you get the message I sent you?"

"I did, although you know I can be a little slow to catch on sometimes. It was actually Alice who found the note in the whistle."

"Alice? Who's Alice?" Silas asked.

"A friend," I said. "She's the sister of Ida, the woman who runs this very boarding house. Alice has been trying to help keep me from getting killed but I think she's finding it to be a tougher job than she'd bargained for." Silas looked at me as if he wasn't sure I was giving him the whole truth about Alice, and maybe I wasn't, but I was eager to get back to learning what had happened to him on the trail.

"Well, I have had quite a time since I left let me tell you." Amid the jams and vegetables, Silas began to tell his story.

CHAPTER 47

"Henry, I don't deny I was pretty darn excited to get going up the Chilkoot. It wasn't the best of circumstances being with Soapy's men but they seemed to know exactly what they were doing. We made good time that first morning, crossing over to Dyea by ferry and as soon as we landed we started the uphill trudge. It wasn't the easiest thing I had ever done, I must say. Everywhere there were horses, mules, and dogs loaded down with prospecting gear along with all manner of men and even a few women trudging along up the trail."

Silas went on, telling me how he'd tried to be friendly with his captors. He'd gotten Ed and Slim to engage in conversation and they seemed pretty happy to have Silas along to help carry the load.

"After about five miles we passed a place called Finnegan's Point but the big stop, Sheep Camp, was still another six miles away. The trail above Finnegan's Point was mighty difficult I must say. If there weren't huge rocks to climb over there were muddy streams clogging up the trail and lots of slippery tree roots, all compounded by the slow-moving caravan of gold seekers." I tried to imagine his first day on the trail and was secretly glad I didn't have to face it.

"Slim said there were only two more miles to Canyon City where some other boys from Soapy's gang would already have set up camp. We made it through a stretch of forest that was thick with undergrowth and even thicker with mosquitoes. When we finally came out into a clearing there was a big river roaring off to our left. It looked like there was a storm approaching, so Ed declared that we probably couldn't make it to Canyon City and we'd make camp at the next flat dry spot we found. As luck would have it we spied a couple of canvas tents already set up on a rise with a campfire blazing.

"There were two men relaxing by the fire and I could smell victuals cooking. Their horses, still loaded down with the rest of their gear, were tethered nearby. We introduced ourselves and those fellas went by names of Hud and Junior. They were mighty friendly and invited us to join them as they had plenty of food and drink for all. It wasn't even dark yet but we were tired so it was a relief to stop before nightfall. We quickly made a makeshift lean-to using cedar branches. We spread tarps out to cover our bedrolls and the campfire smoke helped keep the mosquitoes and flies down as we worked. Secure under cover the rain started up and we dug into large, hot helpings of johnny cakes smothered in beans, compliments of our new friends.

"As we chowed down Junior inquired why we were traveling the Chilkoot route instead of White Pass, which started right in Skaguay. Ed explained that their employer had ordered them to make a cash delivery to a business associate in Sheep Camp. I tell you right then, Henry, I figured out I must be the one hauling around that cash strongbox in my pack. No wonder my load was so heavy!"

Silas said that around the campfire that night, it got to feeling like five lifelong friends swapping stories. Everyone's head was swimming with whiskey and at some point he said Junior pulled out a harmonica and played a few songs. As I listened I'd begun to feel a little envious of his adventures but that was about the last bit of the story that left me feeling that way.

"Along with the drinking and singing," Silas said, "we was all pretty tuckered out from the day so we called it a night and settled into our bedrolls." Silas said it had taken a while for him to fall asleep on account of Junior's thunderous snoring; I didn't mention he had the same problem.

"I'd been having a real nice dream about you and me going back to Seattle in golden suits," Silas said, "when all that whiskey must've worked its way through me and I woke up needing to pee something fierce. I got out of my bedroll and walked down a slope toward the river where I found a tree that looked suitable for taking care of my business. In the moonlight that's when I saw Rags trotting up from the river. She was soaking wet but real friendly and rubbed right up against my trouser leg. She tried to shake herself dry but only succeeded in covering me in muddy splatters. The sight of this poor animal really tugged at my heartstrings so I decided to lead her back up to the camp where she could dry off by the fire and fill her belly with some of the dinner scraps.

"I was walking up the hill, just hopin' the fellas wouldn't be too sore about me inviting a dog to join us when, just as we got far enough to peer over the top of the hill, I saw the worst thing I've ever witnessed in my whole life."

CHAPTER 48

Crouched down with the dog beside him, Silas peered over the hill and said he saw two dark figures silhouetted in the flickering firelight. It was Hud and Junior and they had huge knives in their hands. He watched silently as they moved over to where Slim and Ed were sleeping, threw off their blankets and slit the sleeping men's throats!

"They moved quickly over to my bedroll intent on finishing me off in the same manner, but saw I was gone. They was cussin' and lookin' all around," Silas said, "but in the dark they couldn't see me hiding over the hill. I slipped back down the rise and started to high-tail it toward the river. Lordy, I never was so scared! I was running for my life and kept on running and didn't pay no mind to what I was stepping on, the dog trotting right alongside me."

I was pretty caught up listening to Silas' tale and he was pretty caught up telling it, so we were both startled when the jar we'd used to prop the cellar open suddenly fell into the straw causing the trap door to slam shut. We both held our breath for a few moments and when we didn't hear any footsteps or other noises, Silas slowly pushed the trap door up for a peek. We were relieved to see a cold wet nose snuffling in. He held the door up enough to scratch the dog's head and pulled out a hunk of jerky, tossed it onto the kitchen floor and repositioned the jar. "Now, where was I?"

In his frantic escape from Hud and Junior he said that he and

Rags had the fires of Canyon City in sight but Silas' bare feet couldn't take any more of the rocky terrain. It had started to rain so he decided to stop and huddle up under a rotted out nurse tree. Exhausted, he dozed off.

"When I woke up, there was something furry pressed up against me licking my face," he chuckled.

"Rags was ready to get back on the trail?" I asked.

"No, it wasn't Rags. It was a native woman! Or, rather, it was her dog licking my face. She was leading a mule along the trail, must have spied me looking pretty pathetic and followed her dog over to get a closer look. That's when I woke up mighty scared I'll tell you.

"After a few moments I could tell she meant me no harm, plus her dog and my new dog were being friendly so I stood up and smiled. Her mule was loaded down with several huge burlap bags plus an assortment of pelts draped over it all and I watched as she took one of the bags off and held the mule steady indicating she wanted me to climb onto the remaining cargo. Carrying one bag herself, she led Rags and me around the settlement at Canyon City and all the way up to Sheep Camp. It took until after daybreak and I was so thankful to be riding rather than walking in my ripped up socks. We didn't speak very much and she kept her eyes ahead watching the trail."

"So you've been at Sheep Camp for the past week?" I asked. "When they brought Ed and Slim's bodies into town, I thought for sure you were a goner."

"Sheep Camp is a muddy mess and it makes Skaguay look like San Francisco, but I'd still say I made out the best of the three. I was so lucky that night because if Rags hadn't distracted me for a few minutes, I would have ended up marching right into the middle of a massacre."

Puzzled I asked Silas, "If Sunny found you that first night, why did she tell me she hadn't seen you when I met her a few days later?"

"I'd guess she was trying to protect me," Silas said. "I told her about the murders and that the men who did it were looking for me—to finish the job. Sunny asked me to describe you Henry, just to make sure you were someone she could trust."

"Silas, do you have any idea how that pepperbox gun of yours, the one from your dad, ended up back in Skaguay? It was used to kill that elixir peddler, Mr. Addleson."

"Well, the gun was in my boot like always, and I figured I could quickly answer the call of nature without putting my boots on. Last time I saw them they were still sitting by my bedroll. What with Hud and Junior waving around their knives, I just didn't think it was a good time fetch 'em."

"Then I guess it was Hud and Junior who brought the gun to Skaguay," I said. "And that old coot Snuffy we met in Doc's tent the first day we got here … well, he spread the word that it was your gun. So in addition to Hud and Junior wanting you dead, there is the added problem that Soapy Smith suspects you of another murder here in town and he's offered a reward that has pretty much every soul in Skaguay on the lookout for you."

"Soapy thinks I killed somebody in Skaguay too? He thinks I killed three people?" Silas started shaking his head. "So that man sitting out front of the boarding house with the rifle …"

"I believe he's there to make sure you don't sneak into town and that I don't sneak out."

At that moment, the root cellar door above us slammed shut again. The jar tumbled and landed on something harder than straw. It shattered. Silas pushed the trap door open and started to scold Rags for sticking her nose in.

"Rags, I …" Only this time it wasn't the dog looking down at us.

"Hi Alice," I said.

"Hi Henry." She was carrying a lantern and had the kitchen hatchet in her other hand.

"Alice, this is Silas. We're gonna need your help."

CHAPTER 49

I spent a few nervous hours waiting for Alice to return. She and Silas had left the boarding house around 1:00 am with Rags in tow. Alice in an oilskin coat and oversized man's hat from off the rack in the dining room and Silas without his original disguise but with my hat on to hide his hair. Our plan was for them to pass as just two sourdoughs out on the streets of Skaguay. We figured they needed the charade to work only as long as it took them to reach our hoped-for hiding place three blocks away. In the darkness they should encounter little more than roaming dogs and a handful of stumbling customers coming from the bars. We knew that Soapy's guard could see up and down Broadway so the two would have to pass as drunken fellows wobbling home from the saloon.

They were very successful at this ruse, Alice told me when she returned, and quicker than not were across Broadway onto Third Avenue out of view from any potential onlookers. Their next obstacle was breaking into the hideout without arousing any suspicions.

"Oh my, Henry, I was even more afraid pulling the boards off the back door than I had been walking across Broadway," Alice said. We were whispering in the kitchen waiting for the water to boil for the morning coffee.

"I was sure we would be heard. Fortunately it only took three hard yanks and the doorway was free. Silas pushed it open and the three of us climbed over the remaining slats. Once inside I lit the candle we'd brought along and kept as far away from the front window as we could."

"But you said it was boarded up didn't you?"

"Yes, Soapy had his men nail sturdy planks up to cover the doors and window the day after poor Mr. Addleson's body was found. Even so, I was worried that any light might betray our presence, so I shielded the candle with my hand. But as long as Silas is careful he should be able to avoid being discovered. Just to be extra cautious we decided not to leave the candle burning for very long.

"What did the rest of the place look like?"

"It seemed to have been cleaned out of everything of value. There were no chairs or tables and the front counter had only a giant rusty cash register on it. The cash drawer had been pried open and emptied and some of the push keys were damaged; I suppose it was just too big and heavy for anyone to carry away." Alice was beginning to make the morning biscuits but continued in a conspiratorial whisper.

"Silas scanned the area and set up his bedroll underneath the front counter. Rags did a little more sniffing around before she circled twice and settled onto the bedroll, ready to get some shut-eye. Silas seemed a little more relaxed and told me he would be fine until tomorrow night. He smiled, said thank you and I made my way back over to the back door. He blew out the candle as I was climbing over the slats and asked, 'What place is this anyway?' Thankfully he couldn't see my face when I said, 'This is the dead man's store—the man Soapy thinks you killed.'"

CHAPTER 50

"Alice, I'm so glad you were able to tuck Silas away and get back here unnoticed. I was so worried. It's really kind of you to help me and Silas."

Alice looked at me over the bowl of eggs she was whipping up into a froth, drained them into the cast iron skillet and began waltzing them around in the lard.

"Henry, don't be silly. Hand me that pepper shaker please." The kitchen smells reminded me again that I seemed to be perpetually hungry. I fussed with some leftover biscuit flour on the countertop. Alice smiled at me warmly. I smiled back and followed her out into the dining room, clumping along like a tin soldier.

The room was already packed not only with boarders but with those who knew that Ida's was the place to be whenever bacon smells were wafting out the door. I dropped into my chair by the kitchen entry and watched as Alice and Ida made trip after trip, in and out, carrying mounds of food and pots of coffee. During mealtime there usually wasn't a great deal of conversation going on, just the smacking of mouths and clinking of knives and forks. I surveyed my fellow diners as I waited to be served. Alice made sure that I got a full plate and I was just about to dig in when the front door opened and I saw John and Elmer.

Surprised I called to them and they joined me at the table. "Hey, fellows, when did you get back into town?"

"Early this morning, friend," said John. "Glad to find you here—we were just saying that this would be the place you'd be." John pulled out the chair next to me while Elmer dusted off his hat and hung it on a hook behind my head.

"I have great news to tell you," I gushed.

"We'll go first because ours is of the bad news variety. We spent all day and night and part of the next day looking for your friend Silas, "Elmer shook his head.

"No, wait …" I tried to interrupt.

"No Henry," said John, "we went up as far as Sheep Camp where we met some people who had seen a red-headed man, but we still couldn't locate him. There were so many people and tents up there that we finally just gave up and came back down. Sorry we couldn't help you out." John had received a cup of coffee from Alice and took a gulp. He signaled to her to bring two of the breakfast specials.

"I'm sorry you fellas had to go all the way up to Sheep Camp looking for Silas. Come to find out he was headed back here already!"

They looked at me for a moment then Elmer said, "No skin off our knees, Henry. We are just glad your friend is okay. He is okay isn't he? Where is he? I'd like to meet this fellow!"

"Sorry, Silas isn't here," I said. "We wouldn't dare have him out in plain sight what with Soapy and his gang gunning for him."

"What in the Sam Hill are you talking about, Henry?" asked John. "What does Soapy want with Silas?"

"Oh, right, you haven't heard. When the elixir fellow was shot, they found Silas' gun at the scene of the crime. And apparently, Soapy and poor Mr. Addleson were like brothers so now Soapy is hellbent on revenge," I explained.

John swallowed and pointed his empty fork my way. "Say, you haven't told anyone that Silas is back in town have you? Sounds like you'd be in a world of hurt if Soapy knew you knew."

"What? no! It's just me and Alice—and now you two—who even know about Silas' return. Oh and Sunny knows too, seeing as how she was the one who helped him out on the trail. Can I count on you to keep it quiet until we figure out a way to get him out of Skaguay?"

"For sure, Henry, we'll keep your secret. What are friends for if not to keep each other's secrets? But what are you gonna do now?" asked Elmer.

"We haven't quite concocted a plan," I confided, "but we've hidden Silas until all the confusion about his gun and Mr. Addleson's murder gets straightened out."

"Perhaps me and Elmer could help out. You know we're booked on the Emerald Queen leaving tomorrow at high tide."

"That's right, we could smuggle him onboard somehow. Maybe he could hide in a crate, and we could let him out when we got underway," Elmer suggested.

"Good idea, Elmer," John agreed, "what do you think of that plan Henry?"

"That sounds great," I said. "that is so nice of you to help."

"How about you meet us at the Nome later this evening and we'll work out the specifics," said John, "to get Silas stowed on board the ship."

"By the way Henry, where is he hiding anyway?" asked Elmer.

I grinned, "Somewhere no one would think to look."

CHAPTER 51

I needed to take a rest after breakfast because the previous night had been long and sleepless. My body was aching from my encounter with Soapy's thugs so I climbed the stairs and eased down onto my bed hoping for a short nap. I woke up with a start in the late afternoon feeling a sight better for the sleep. When I got back down to the dining room it was empty. Sadly I had missed Ida's delicious lunch service. Possibly I could get something to eat at my rendezvous with John and Elmer so I headed out the front door. My watcher grunted, "Where you off to then?"

"I'm just going up to the Nome to get a bite."

"That's sounds like a fine idea, I think I'll do the same," he smiled and spit out into the street. He shouldered his rifle and made his way ahead of me up the street.

I turned to follow him when someone called out my name. Frank Brown, the bartender from the Denali was standing in front of his establishment waving me over.

"Good day to you Mr. Brown."

"Same to you Henry," Frank said. "Headed out on the town are you?"

"I thought I might meet up with some friends for a drink at the Nome Saloon," I said.

Mr. Brown raised his eyebrows at this. "You know we sell drinks right here at the Denali. Seems like it'd be a sight more convenient for a fellow on crutches." I stared down at the ground trying to figure a way out of this awkward situation. "It's okay. I don't suppose I blame you for preferring an establishment that has more friendly faces and less Soapy Smith." I nodded. "From what I gather, though, you've got a really good friend in Skaguay," he said.

I tried to keep my surprise and worry from showing on my face. How could he know about Silas' return? I'd only told three people. Which of them would be so careless with my secret?

"What do you mean?" I asked.

"Alice, boy! Any fool can see she's really taken a shine to you!" I was relieved to know that he wasn't talking about Silas, but then I was nervous all over again talking about Alice. "I'm assuming you're pretty fond of her too," he grinned slyly, "either that or you just like drinking coffee more than anyone else in Alaska. We see you camped out by that door to the kitchen so much, folks wonder if you even remember that you have a room upstairs."

I joined him in laughing at myself for believing that I'd been inconspicuous about my affection for Alice. "Well, she's a really nice girl," I said.

"Nice?! That Alice is a peach! You ought to be honored that she'd even look at you twice. But I reckon she's a pretty good judge of character. I'm sorry to see that you've got yourself in a bit of a spot at present."

"I'd have to agree with you there," I told him, as I glanced up the street thinking I really ought to be on my way to the Nome meeting by now.

Perhaps sensing my urgency to leave, Mr. Brown said, "Well, you go ahead and get that drink you were planning. I'm sure everything will eventually work out okay."

I thanked him and set off moving as quickly as my limited mobility allowed.

CHAPTER 52

"The trick will be getting Silas out to Juneau Wharf without being seen," John explained as he leaned on the bar at the Nome. "That dock stretches nearly a half mile out into the inlet and there won't be nowhere for Silas to hide along the length of it until the incoming cargo get unloaded. Soapy's got someone following you so you must stay out of sight at Ida's. You don't want to tip 'em off to Silas' location." That made sense to me.

"When will the Emerald Queen be coming in?"

"Oh, she'll be tying up at high tide near ten o'clock tonight. We'll take advantage of all the hubbub of unloading activities to transfer our going-home cargo along with yours," Elmer replied. Knowing that Silas would soon be safely away from Skaguay—and Soapy Smith—made me happy, but I was feeling sad at the thought of being left behind. We were partners in this adventure after all. Then I thought, hey, why don't I buy a ticket and go too?

"Say, what do you think about me buying a passage on the ship and going home to Seattle? There's really nothing here that ..." I looked to my friends who were already shaking their heads.

"Henry, I smell a couple of dead rats floating around that idea," John said. "You're being watched so how in blazes do you think Soapy will allow you to leave pretty as you please? He's not going to give you an escort down to the ship."

"Well, I guess …"

"And don't you think he'd figure out that somehow Silas had slipped through his net and was either on the boat or already made his escape some other way? I mean look Henry, don't be an idiot. You can go home on any other ship after today. I just think you'd be tipping our hand if'n you booked on the same ship your friend's a stowaway on."

"Yep, I agree with John," said Elmer, "if you want to book on a later date we'll lend you the money right now. Friends help friends out you know."

"You're right, you're right. I wasn't thinking clearly," I replied. "I'll wait until I know Silas is safe in Seattle and then I'll make my way back home."

"That's settled, then. Now, to the details …"

The three of us claimed a table and while John went to fetch a round of drinks Elmer pulled out a deck of cards. "Best make like we're having a friendly game while we finalize our plan." He shuffled the cards and dealt out a hand. Just three card players passing the time, that's what we meant to seem like. I looked at my cards. Seemed I'd been dealt aces and eights—dead man's hand.

"Will you be able to get to Silas' hiding place by yourself?" murmured Elmer. "What with Soapy's watcher over there?" He tossed his head in the direction of my current guard; I didn't look up.

"That's the beauty of it, I won't be going to collect Silas! Oh, did I tell you he has a dog too? That shouldn't be a problem, should it? Anyway, I will be acting as a decoy–I'll leave the boarding house and head up Broadway luring the guard to follow me. Then Alice will hurry over to tell Silas where to hide down by the wharf. Genius, don't you think?" I leaned back in my chair proud of my contribution to the plan.

"Dash-fire!" exclaimed Elmer, "how did your friend end up with a dog? I think that dog may add an unnecessary wrinkle in our plans. Can't he just leave it behind?" Both John and Elmer stared at me shaking their heads, "It's just a dog."

"I'm pretty sure Silas won't leave the dog behind because that dog actually saved his life. He found it, or rather they found each other when he escaped from the murderers. If not for Rags, he would have been killed right along with the other two. He was able to see the killers, though, didn't I tell you that? Gadzooks, it was something! I was scared just listening to his tale." I had both John and Elmer's undivided attention now.

"Yep, he said he had to answer a call of nature and that dog just trotted up and made friends right then and there. Silas loves animals and when he and the dog were working their way back up the bank towards camp, the dog heard—and probably smelled—the attack. It was that dog that kept Silas from getting his throat cut so I'm guessing the dog goes along with him when he comes out of hiding later tonight."

Elmer and John reached for their beers and downed them. "Another round?" asked John. "This one's on Elmer!" John's chair scraped across the wooden floor. He slapped me on the back as he passed. "Don't say nothin' else 'til I get back friend."

CHAPTER 53

It was the tail end of dinner by the time I got back to the boardinghouse. Alice suspected I might not make it back in time for food, so she'd gone ahead and set aside a plate for me. While the last of the other patrons finished up Alice sat down at my table and leaned in, "So what do you need me to do?"

I explained John and Elmer's plan for helping Silas stow away on the Emerald Queen. Alice was none too keen on a plan that relied on them, but like me, she couldn't come up with any better idea for getting Silas out of Skaguay without being discovered. She agreed that once she'd cleaned up for the evening she'd sneak back over to Addleson's elixir store and let Silas know the escape plan: get down to Juneau Wharf by midnight. John and Elmer would be there to help Silas hide in one of the many crates being loaded for the voyage to Seattle.

"And your friends said that it was okay for Silas to bring Rags along?" Alice asked.

"Well, they didn't say he couldn't bring her. I think they'd prefer the dog stay behind, but once I'd explained about Rags saving Silas' life, I think they understood that it had to be this way."

"Hey Alice, I need your help in here," Ida called out from the kitchen.

"After I finish helping Ida I'll go and let Silas know what he needs to do." Alice turned toward the kitchen, but then looked back at me.

"You know Henry, I keep thinking that a smarter gal wouldn't let herself get tangled up in this mess."

I smiled and thought to myself that I had no idea how I'd manage without her help. "You're a peach, Alice."

I watched as she disappeared into the kitchen then turned toward the front window of the boarding house and saw Soapy's watchman glowering directly at me. Another man from the gang was leaning over whispering to him, but my guard kept his eyes locked on me. He had probably been staring at Alice and me the entire time we were talking. If he put two and two together he'd be suspicious enough to want to keep an eye on us both. When Alice returned a few minutes later, I told her that she'd need to sneak out through the kitchen to avoid being detected by Soapy's men out front. She untied her apron and draped it over the back of a chair and said, "I don't think it'll be a problem, there isn't anyone out there."

Confused, I turned and saw that Alice was right. The chair that had been occupied since my near drowning was empty. My stomach was in knots. The plan had to work. Unsure why my guard had suddenly disappeared we decided to hurry out before he returned. Alice took off to inform Silas and I soon found myself next door at the Denali bar. Frank smiled and walked over to me. "Hey Henry, didn't you say you'd be patronizing the Nome this evening?"

"Well, I heard a rumor that maybe this place also sells drinks, so I thought I'd give it a try," I laughed.

"No complaints from me. I could use more customers."

"Yeah," I said, looking around the barroom, "seems like the crowd in here is kinda sparse. D'ya suppose the people of Skaguay aren't thirsty tonight?"

Frank shook his head. "There was a decent sized crowd earlier, but then Soapy came in and lit a fire under his boys ordering them off somewhere."

The knots in my stomach gripped tighter. "Where to?" I asked.

"Seems there was something going on down at the wharf that needed their attention."

CHAPTER 54

Shocked, I'd tried to move for the door of the Denali but Frank had come from behind the bar to block my path. "Henry, where you going in such a rush?"

"I'm sorry, Frank. I can't tell you that."

"You know how to fire a pistol?" Frank asked.

"Um, yeah, I guess."

"Well, then take this along."

"No, I couldn't ta—" I sputtered but Frank grabbed my left hand and slapped a revolver into my palm. He looked me dead in the eye, "Anything that has a fellow in such a godawful panic is bound to require a weapon better than that crutch you've got. Take this Colt."

I hobbled past Second Street toward the lights flickering down at Juneau Wharf with the unfamiliar weight of a gun tucked into my belt. Just as John and Elmer had assured me the Emerald Queen was now docked, so our plan of getting Silas out of Skaguay and out of Soapy Smith's reach was underway. Even if Soapy's men were already down there I knew that John and Elmer would take pains to keep Silas hidden until the most opportune moment to get him onboard. I was thankful for their friendship as I could not have been so creative.

The first several steps along the planks of the pier were still reassuringly illuminated by the glow of the town behind me but as I ventured further, I found myself in moonlit shadows. Most of the light was eclipsed by the stacks of wooden crates, barrels, sacks of mail, and pounds of equipment all towering above me on both sides of the wharf. I took another couple of tentative steps but jerked to a halt when I heard a creaking noise. Standing still, holding my breath, I heard a whooshing in my ears in rhythm with my heartbeat. "He— Hello?" I asked, the effort getting lodged in my throat. No response, then the creaking again, followed by a scritch, scratch sound. I grabbed the revolver and brought it up slowly in front of me. My hand trembled as I positioned my thumb over the hammer of the pistol.

"Henr— Henry, what in tarnation?!?" exclaimed a wide-eyed Silas staring at the pistol barrel. He stepped out from behind a stack of crates to my right with Alice behind him. Rags sprung up on me gleefully pinning me up against a crate with her front paws on my chest. I lowered the gun and leaned heavily on my crutch taking in deep breaths to get my nerves back under control.

"Silas, Alice, I'm so relieved to see you." Rags dropped down and started pacing.

"Henry, why do you have a gun?" asked Alice.

"It's not mine. When I stopped by the Denali, Mr. Brown told me Soapy was rounding up his boys to head down here. Frank saw how spooked I was so he insisted I bring this along."

"Soapy's down here?" Alice asked looking around.

"I'm not sure," I said. "But the sooner John and Elmer can get Silas hidden in with their cargo the better. You haven't seen them yet have you?"

"No, we've been looking for the crates with those marks like you told me, but there's barely enough light to see anything," Alice said. Earlier at the Nome, John and Elmer had explained that they'd stacked four large wooden crates on the right side of the pier about 100 yards shy of where ships normally moored. Three of the crates were filled with their Seattle-bound belongings but in the fourth crate they'd left enough room for Silas to hide. Not comfortably, they said, but it would be sufficient until the ship was clear of the harbor and Silas could come out in the open. They said they'd meet up with Silas at the crates they'd marked with two parallel slashes of green paint.

I agreed with Alice that it was going to be tough to make out any markings without more light, so I figured I'd light a match just for a second. As I was fumbling for matches, Rags barked loudly, and the matches scattered in the wind. Even without any extra light it was Alice who first spied the green markings when Rags uttered a low, menacing growl.

"Shhhh!! Rags, keep quiet," I scolded. The dog hunkered down but continued with a guttural, itching-for-a-fight sound.

"You're sure your friends said midnight?" Silas asked.

"Yep. They oughta be here by now."

CHAPTER 55

"**D**o you think maybe they forgot about me?" asked Silas. Rags continued to growl.

"We most definitely did not forget about you Silas." It was Elmer's voice coming from behind me. I squinted but did not see him immediately. Slowly his face came into view as he took a couple of strides toward us.

"Hey Elmer, there you are, where's John?" I asked.

In answer to my question, I heard John say, "Over here, Henry."

Turning I saw Silas and Alice take a step backwards toward me. When John emerged, the light from the ship was at his back putting his face mostly in shadows.

"Hey, Silas, I said, "these are my friends John and Elmer."

"No, Henry … it's not." Silas said, his voice shaky. "They're Hud and Junior."

Rags' growling continued unabated and I struggled to make sense of what was happening. I started to correct Silas—to explain to him that these were the guys with the plan, that they were going to make sure he got out of Skaguay alive. But then I saw the black steel revolver extended in John's hand. I turned to see that Elmer had a gun drawn as well and it was aimed directly at me.

"Henry, you weren't supposed to be here," said Elmer. Although it must've been plainly obvious to everyone there, I still felt compelled to say, "I don't understand."

"Honestly friend, we can't leave town without tying up loose ends," said Elmer, "and Silas here, he's our one loose end."

John added, "He's been our unfinished business ever since that night on the Chilkoot trail when he managed to be missing from his bedroll at the time his companions met their unfortunate fate."

"You mean when you murdered them," Silas said.

John had his gun trained on Silas so I swung around to point Mr. Brown's Colt at John but he quickly locked one arm around Alice's neck and put the gun to her head. "Sure, sure call it what you wish," said John. "Henry, we both know you aren't really gonna do anything with that gun so why don't you put it on the ground and Elmer and I just might consider letting you and your pretty girlfriend here go."

Even I knew that was a lie. Elmer and John had no intention of leaving any witnesses. Mind racing, I tried desperately to think of a way out of this standoff when I saw Alice staring intently at me. It wasn't the fearful expression that I'd expected to see—more like a determined look. Then I noticed she was clutching something tightly by her side. Right then I knew I wasn't going to be following John's command to put the gun down. I cocked the revolver and in one swift movement Alice raised her fist and punched her 16 penny protection nail into John's thigh. He screamed and clawed at the spike protruding from his leg allowing Alice to twist free. I fired and hit John squarely in the chest. The blast was immediately followed by something slamming against the back of my head. The gun, knocked from my hand, clattered across the wooden planks.

"That was stupid, Henry," Elmer said staring down at me. "Now I'm afraid I'll have to kill you along with your friends."

I assumed this was the end, but Rags had other ideas. She leapt at Elmer knocking him to the ground. While man and dog struggled, Silas, Alice, and I fled toward the ship. With the two of them on either side of me we reached the gangway to the Emerald Queen. Silas helped me up the steep incline. We were almost to the top of the ramp where hopefully we'd have more options for safety. Maybe even someone could help protect us but the few men on deck just stared at us, then moved aside. Soapy Smith stood in the dim light armed with a smirk and a shotgun.

"No, Soapy!" I sputtered. "Silas had nothing to do with the murders."

"I know that," Soapy replied calmly. "I'm not here for your friend. Do you wanna tell them 'Hud', or shall I?" Soapy's gaze shifted down onto the dock. There was Elmer at the bottom of the gangway bleeding from his hand and shoulder. He still wielded a gun and had a wild look in his eyes.

"You see," Soapy said, "Hud here was an associate of our dearly departed friend Mr. Addleson, during their younger days back in Seattle."

Elmer—or Hud, as Soapy was calling him—aimed his gun directly at Soapy. His target, however, held his shotgun steady and still seemed strangely at ease.

"Henry, I hate that you got caught up with this criminal element," Soapy said.

"Ha!" scoffed Elmer. "Soapy Smith? As if there is any bigger criminal than you."

"I'm hardly a choir boy but I am not a murderer, Hud," Soapy replied.

"Not a murderer?" said Elmer. "Seems you've got a gun on me and I've got a gun on you so I can't rightly see what difference there is between you 'n me."

"The difference?" Soapy said as his scowl slowly broadened into a cold grin, the same one I'd seen the day he'd just about killed me in the street. "The difference Hud, is that I have many friends in Skaguay who don't mind cleaning up scum like you."

With those words a barrage of bullets was unleashed from the darkness and the man I'd known as Elmer fell to the ground, dead, a bloody pool forming around him.

CHAPTER 56

Long afternoon shadows stretched across the floor in the dining room. The usual aromas had drawn patrons in but I lacked any appetite for food. Alice sat down for a moment and said, "Henry, you don't have to be upset about what happened, those guys didn't give you any choice."

"Yeah, Henry," Silas added, "you shooting that guy is the only reason we all made it out of there alive."

"Rags might be better off, though," I said flatly. We looked over at the pile of blankets arranged in a corner near the front door. That night on the dock, while we raced toward the Emerald Queen, Rags fought on valiantly. We heard a gunshot and a splash but couldn't see anything. Once it was all over and John and Elmer lay dead we went looking for her but in the darkness couldn't find her. Vowing to resume the search at daybreak we made our way back to the boarding house and happily discovered a soaking wet, shivering Rags waiting on the front porch! Silas ran to her and saw she was oozing blood from a gunshot wound so he swooped her up and got busy tending her wounds.

"You kidding me?" Frank Brown interjected pulling up a chair to join the three of us at my favorite table by the kitchen door. "That dog's been eating her weight in moose jerky and everyone who comes in dotes on her like she's royalty. Rags probably thinks that when she fell off that pier she landed in canine heaven."

"I think so too," said Silas smiling over at his friend, "but I'm worried about Henry. It's been three days and he still seems rattled."

"I don't understand," said Alice, "everything worked out for the best."

"I figure Henry knows it worked out the best it could, ain't that right, Henry? But that's not the point. You ever killed a man?" Frank asked Alice. She shook her head. "What about you, Silas? You ever took a man's life?"

"No sir," Silas said.

"Well, it changes a fella. Don't matter if the killin' was for the right reason or the wrong reason," Frank said.

"You've killed somebody before?" Silas asked.

Frank nodded solemnly. "War between the States. Did things I never wanted to do. Saw things no one should ever have to see."

"How long did it take before you got better?" asked Alice, glancing over at me.

"Better?" Frank asked. "When the war was finally over, I tried going back to my life in Michigan but I never got to feeling better. Eventually I just gave up and headed west. That made it more bearable, but you can never really outrun your memor—"

At that moment, the front door flew open and in walked a man we hadn't laid eyes on since that night, the man who had become our rescuer, Soapy Smith.

CHAPTER 57

Instead of having his usual lackeys in tow, Soapy Smith was accompanied by the lumberjack brothers, Howard and Matthew Guthrie. Matthew's neck and the lower part of his face were covered by either a particularly nasty rash or he'd been attacked by a swarm of bees. The three men surveyed the boarding house dining area; Howard leaned over to pat Rags while Soapy tossed a hunk of dried meat down on the blankets. Rags sniffed this latest offering and put her head back down.

"Well now, looks like the gang's all here," Soapy roared, "let me buy everyone a drink." He held up a full bottle of whiskey. He sat at an empty table and beckoned for us to join them. Alice fetched a tray of shot glasses and Frank Brown took the bottle and did what he does best: pour drinks for all takers.

Soapy raised his glass and the rest of us followed suit as he offered a toast, "To friendship, Skaguay, and good riddance to those two murderous scoundrels." We clinked glasses and downed the whiskey. Though Soapy was as jovial as I'd ever seen him, I still felt uneasy in his presence. There were so many questions I wanted to have answered but I was nervous about asking unsure where to begin.

Alice didn't share my reservations. "Soapy, seemed like you were all set on getting back at Silas for killing those men," Alice blurted, "so how'd you figure out that Silas wasn't the murderer?"

"Well, as I told you that night on the dock, them two ruffians was business partners of Hiram Addleson from his days in Seattle. Seems they come up to Alaska bearing a grudge over this or that," Soapy said. "They also come up here bearing this," Soapy reached into his inside coat pocket and unfolded what appeared to be a printed advertisement which he spread out on the table. The advertisement was for a Seattle business called Dunnam Woolens that outfitted prospectors for journeying north. *GOLD, GOLD, GOLD!!!* was printed across the top of the page. In the middle of the advertisement was a photo of grizzled but grinning men which was captioned *Dyea, Alaska 1897*. There in the photo, third smiling man from the right, stood Mr. Hiram Addleson.

"The man you called John had that," Soapy said, pointing at the paper, "in his pocket when you gunned him down."

"I don't understand. You're saying they saw this picture of their old business partner in Seattle and decided to come here kill him?" I was confused.

Soapy lit up a cigar. When he had a good ash going he continued, "Well the thing is they would've come to kill him sooner, excepting they thought he was already dead."

CHAPTER 58

"Already dead?" Alice asked.

Soapy went on to explain that Hiram and his two partners had operated a business down near the waterfront in Seattle. "One night a fire broke out, and it happened to be a night when there was a considerable amount of cash in the building and Hiram was working late," Soapy explained. "The building was pretty shoddy construction and went up quickly in a terrible conflagration, in minutes the whole thing had burned to the ground. All they recovered from the ashes were the remains of one Hiram Addleson. The story in the Seattle newspaper identified him as a real family man and pillar of the community," Soapy chuckled.

"But it wasn't really Mr. Addleson who perished in the fire?" Silas asked.

"Don't see how it could've been since he popped up in Skaguay a few weeks later with a considerable amount of cash. I know this because he approached me wanting to invest in a venture that would pay huge dividends for the both of us."

"So he faked his death and fled Seattle with John and Elmer's money?" I asked. Soapy gave me a sideways glance, cleared his throat and went on with his story.

"So when Mr. Hiram Addleson was gunned down like a dog, no offense Rags, you can bet I was damn mad! He was not only a friend but an integral part of our business here and over in Dawson City."

At that point in Soapy's story, Ida came out from the kitchen and stood behind me with her hand resting on my chair.

"And what business exactly was it you and Addleson was so invested in? Certainly it wasn't the potions and elixir trade!" said Ida. For some unknown reason, Ida seemed to be able to talk rather bluntly to Soapy. The rest of us certainly would never think to be so bold.

"Ah, dear Ida, you know perfectly well what business," Soapy said without any malice, "your boarding house here will benefit, as will the rest of the town. You can't deny that can you?"

"No, Soapy I can't deny that a new railroad line right down the center of town will benefit Alice and me greatly. I can only hope that everyone who has been a party to all the dealings is as satisfied as you seem to be." Ida wiped her hands on her apron and started to pick up the glasses from the table.

"Leave them be, woman," Soapy said, "we ain't done drinking to everyone's good fortunes yet."

"Flames to your good fortunes," Ida mumbled and went back into her kitchen.

"There's gonna be a railroad coming through Skaguay?" Silas asked.

"Big business interests down south are itching to get in on the gold rush action," said Soapy, "but they aren't too keen on hauling a ton of supplies over the mountains every time they want to look for some gold. Word got out that the railroad was either gonna run through Dyea or through Skaguay with the chosen location a boom town and the town they don't pick becomes a ghost town."

"And they picked Skaguay?" Alice asked.

"Well, it warn't looking very good for us; that's when I dispatched Ed and Slim, along with Silas here, to get to the railroad men before they made their decision," Soapy explained. "We wanted the railroad interests to know there was good reason to choose Skaguay even though they were leaning toward Dyea as the railhead."

"What was the good reason?" Silas asked.

Soapy told us that he sent Ed and Slim in possession of 20,000 good reasons to be delivered post haste to the railroad friends to help them make a favorable decision.

CHAPTER 59

T hough upset about the murders, Soapy was particularly incensed that someone had absconded with his twenty thousand dollars. Whoever had killed Ed and Slim had jeopardized the future of his Skaguay railroad interests.

"So you thought Silas had stolen the money?" Alice asked.

"Yes, for a time I suspected exactly that, because Ed and Slim's corpses turned up a few days after leaving in your company," Soapy said, turning to look at Silas, "so you can see why I had to try to persuade your friend Henry to tell me where you was hiding." My mind flashed back to the day when his "persuasion" tactics were, sure as shooting, going to result in my demise.

"Sorry 'bout that boy," Soapy shrugged his shoulders, "but you were the only likely person to know anything and if Snuffy hadn't put two and two together about that tiny gun, I'd never have suspected your friend at all for Addleson's murder." Soapy reached for the whiskey bottle and refilled everyone's glass. "When Henry wouldn't tell me what I needed to know, I assumed he was either too loyal to care about the consequences or too stupid to know any better." I heard a soft chortle from Alice. "I dispatched some of my men to find Silas; figured it couldn't be that hard to locate a fella with fiery hair like that. What my men soon learned however, was that they were not the first people to come a-lookin' around the Chilkoot for him. Word was there were a couple of other guys who'd been asking around Sheep Camp, real eager to find him. Just so happens that I have a reliable friend at Sheep Camp and she was sure those other men looked very familiar. She'd seen 'em hanging around Nome Saloon back here in Skaguay."

"Was it Sunny who saw them? Sunny is one of your friends?!" Silas asked excitedly.

"Just listen and don't interrupt," Soapy smiled.

"But you did say 'she' recognized those men!"

"I'm sure I said no such thing," Soapy said, snubbing out the end of his cigar. "As I was saying … when my reliable source tipped me off to Hud and Junior, I ordered my men to tail them. When they reported seeing Hud and Junior moving crates onto the wharf and then going back into Skaguay, I reckoned some sort of escape plan was underway. The best vantage point would be from the deck of the Emerald Queen so we boarded her to lie in wait. No way would them two thieving killers get away from Soapy Smith! Since Hud and Junior had no idea I was wise to 'em, we'd capture 'em red-handed when they returned to load up their cargo. The involvement of you three, plus Rags over there, complicated things a wee bit. But I have to thank you for serving as unwitting decoys in our little hunting foray. And Henry, quicker'n lightning, you went from hunted to hunter and saved the day, finished off one of them murdering scoundrels and flushed the other right into my clutches." So that's all I was—a decoy.

"You all know the rest—when we busted open those crates not only was the railroad cash in there but also a goodly amount of the dearly departed's personal belongings. Them varmints even stole the widows and orphans collection coins and that's about as low as a thief can get."

Soapy shook his head. "But, all's well that ends well, right? And, it now seems that the railroad folks have found my arguments in favor of Skaguay most compelling, which means we're sitting pretty right in the middle of a boomtown. Also, I've made a substantial investment in the first steam-powered sawmill in the area and the Guthrie brothers here are gonna run it. They'll be needing some help, of course. You interested?"

"That's kind of you, Mr. Smith …" I began.

"Call me Soapy."

"Okay … Soapy. That's mighty kind of you. But me and Silas came up here to seek our fortune in gold and then head back to Seattle."

Soapy slowly turned his head, appraising the face of each person seated at our table. "Henry, make no mistake," he said, "there's a fortune to be made in this gold rush, but it ain't the yellow metal that holds the key to it. Sure, a couple of happy idiots will go home with nuggets enough to spend a few years wearin' fancy suits and sipping good whiskey, but most of them dopes headed over the mountains will come back with little more than a frostbitten pecker to show for it. Them that even make it back, that is." Soapy struck a match to fire up another of his thin cigars then continued. "And besides, what sort of life you got waiting for you back in Seattle? You got a girl? A family? Any sort of prospects for the future?"

CHAPTER 60

I've heard that sometimes the truth hurts and I'd have to say this was one of those times. Soapy was right about us not having much reason to hurry back to Seattle. It was the lack of prospects back home that had made setting off for the Klondike such an easy choice in the first place.

"We sure are gonna need help with the lumber operation," Matthew Guthrie chimed in. "Hope you fellas will at least consider coming to work at the new mill." At that, Soapy stood up, and the Guthrie brothers followed suit.

"Boys, I'm sure Silas and Henry will come to realize what a great opportunity this is for them," Soapy said. "What I wouldn't give to be your age with all life's adventures ahead of me." The three men tipped their hats to Alice, and to Ida, who had just emerged from the kitchen to gather the glasses, and made their way out the front door.

"What do you think Henry?" Silas asked.

"I think Soapy slipped up and let us know that Sunny is one of his spies," I replied.

At that comment Ida laughed out loud. "You two are real nice and all but you're dumber'n dishwater. Soapy don't let nothin' 'slip' so if that man gives you anything you can be sure he was meaning for you to have it, and you'll be paying him back somehow."

"It seems like working with the Guthries could be a great opportunity for you," Frank said.

Silas grinned, "Especially if Henry can manage to keep his fingers out of the saw!"

My friend leaned over to me and in a conspiratorial whisper assured me that it was "going to be great!"

I looked across the room where Rags lay, gnawing away on the gift of dried meat Soapy had bestowed upon her. I thought about the people around the table and about how kind they had been to me. As slow as I can be sometimes, I knew staying in Skaguay would work out for us.

"Yeah, Silas. You're right," I said. "It *is* going to be great."

ACKNOWLEDGMENTS

The author wishes to acknowledge the following people for their help in bringing this story to life: Matthew, the only person allowed to read the very first draft; Kristy Alley and Craig Abramson for providing crucial feedback on the manuscript; Eowyn Ivey and the much-missed Brian Doyle for their generous support and insight at North Words Writers Symposium; Susannah Dowds, historian extraordinaire, for diligently digging up resources and answering my many questions at the Klondike Gold Rush National Historical Park—I hope I've avoided too many cringeworthy inaccuracies; the wonderfully talented Jason Reynolds who shared his wisdom over lunch after he'd rendered an auditorium packed with middle-schoolers entirely spellbound; and Skaguay News Depot and Books, for keeping the original "U" in Skaguay, despite the tyranny of the post office and auto-correct.

ABOUT THE AUTHOR

Martin Stroud has been crafting suspense and adventure short stories for many years, but research for one such story led to his first novel, *Scoundrels of Skaguay*. Martin enjoys travel to quirky locales, grueling nature hikes, energy bars, and playing with his two dogs, Jocko and Hitch. He splits his time between Seattle & Memphis: Hendrix & Stax, Kurt & Sun, salmon & BBQ, majestic mountains & The Mighty Mississippi.

Made in the USA
Middletown, DE
22 July 2019